INFECTION CONTROL

Breaking the Rules

by

P. V. Smith

DORRANCE PUBLISHING CO
EST. 1920
PITTSBURGH, PENNSYLVANIA 15222

The contents of this work, including, but not limited to, the accuracy of events, people, and places depicted; opinions expressed; permission to use previously published materials included; and any advice given or actions advocated are solely the responsibility of the author, who assumes all liability for said work and indemnifies the publisher against any claims stemming from publication of the work.

Dorrance Publishing Co
701 Smithfield Street
Pittsburgh, PA 15222
Visit our website at *www.dorrancebookstore.com*

ISBN: 978-1-4809-0957-1
eISBN: 978-1-4809-0819-2

This book is dedicated to the following:

To my husband, Neville, with whom I have weathered many storms. You have always been my rock, standing strong beside me. Thank you for your unwavering love.

To Patricia, my daughter. I am intensely proud of the woman and mother you've become. God does answer prayer.

To Casey, my son. You are more wonderful than you give yourself credit for. You are kind, generous, and a gentleman in every sense of the word. Don't change.

To Jaime, my grandson. Stay sweet. The world will be a better place for having you in it.

To Jasmin, my granddaughter. You bring light into every dark corner. Stay beautiful, and may you continue to shine as long as God gives you breath.

To Mrs. Joyce Dixon, my New York mom. Thanks for all the kindness you have shown to me and my family over the years. You took me under your wings and mentored me when I first arrived in this country as a young and inexperienced nurse. You have treated us like family, and words are inadequate to tell you how grateful I am. I love you like a mom and a friend, and I will never ever forget all your kindness.

To my brother and sisters-in-law. You have welcomed me into the family with open arms and without reservation. Pam, Silma, and Jennifer, you are the sisters I never had, and I love and appreciate you all.

Last, but by no means least, to my former coworkers—you know who you are. We had some good times and some tough times, but we always managed to hang together. There was always strength in our unity, and the camaraderie contributed to making things more tolerable.

God bless as you continue your tireless endeavor in the pursuit of that ever-evasive organism.

Happy bug hunting!

Acknowledgments

John Donne said it so eloquently: "No man is an island, entire of itself; every man is a piece of the continent, a part of the main...."

To the following individuals, without whom this book would never have been written. You are all a part of this effort; I could not have done this all by myself.

First, to my husband, Neville, who always believed I had a story to tell, even when I never believed I did. Thanks for his encouragement and patience. He always believed in me even when I felt like giving up so many times.

To my children, Patricia and Casey, their encouragement meant so much to me. I'm extremely proud of you both.

To my friends, Joan and Patricia, who acted as my impartial readers/advisors. Thanks for your positive criticisms and for your input as members of the profession. May you continue to be honest and open with me always.

To the members of Writers of Light, the Hebron Baptist Church writing group. When I first brought this to you as a short story, you told me you wanted more. Thanks for that push; there was indeed more to tell.

Last but not least, to my editor, Aneisha Lopez, for your patience, unfailing guidance, editing, and encouragement. May your lamp continue to burn ever so brightly, and may God continue to bless you in all your endeavors.

Introduction

Infection Control: Breaking the Rules is the story of one of the most important and essential departments that exists in today's healthcare facilities: It is the Infection Control Department. Ask anyone on the street if they know about the infection control department in their local hospital, and they will most likely say they never heard of it. Obscure as it may sound, this department is responsible for preventing and controlling myriads of infections throughout healthcare facilities. Because of the quick decisions made by these infection crime fighters, many lives have been saved.

This book is a humorous view of a very serious subject: preventing and controlling the spread of infection. It is a view of how life could be in a large medical center through the eyes of the author. The story is based on the author's experience as a registered nurse for over forty years, the last fifteen of which were spent as an infection control nurse.

References to real people, events, establishments, organizations, or locations are intended only to provide a sense of authenticity and are used fictitiously. They are the product of the author's imagination, and any resemblance between actual persons living or dead is purely coincidental.

Every effort has been made to ensure that references are correct; *however, this book is not intended to be used as a reference of any kind.* The characters are very human. They laugh, they cry, they have secrets, and they suffer from feelings that we all encounter. Overall, they appeal to our emotions as human beings while allowing a brief look into their private lives, and they often times remind us of ourselves.

In *Infection Control: Breaking The Rules*, the infection control team consists of dedicated and driven nurses that hail from different parts of the world: the United States, Philippines, Jamaica, and Antigua. Thus, the racial mix is very diverse and makes for very interesting interaction.

The two main characters are Natalie Sinclair and Brandon Saunders. Natalie Sinclair is the product of an interracial marriage. She had a very unhappy childhood, but has survived and escapes to the bright lights of New York City, where she finds her niche and the happiness she has craved. She loves her job as director of Infection Control at Justice Medical Center, but she is dealing with some health issues that might bring her career to a halt.

Brandon Saunders is the hospital administrator. He is ambitious, conniving, and will do whatever it takes to take over the helm of the prestigious New York City Public Regional Hospitals System. However, he has some secrets that have been kept very well hidden for a long time. These secrets are about to be exposed, and he will do everything in his power for this not to happen.

Natalie Sinclair

This Monday morning was no different from any other at Justice Medical Center in the Bronx, New York. It was the middle of January. The thermometer was heading steadily toward zero. Natalie Sinclair hunched her shoulders against the biting wind as she struggled from the parking lot and headed for her office.

The cold was so intense it brought tears to her eyes. Justice, as many affectionately called it, was situated in the northeast portion of the county. On this morning, there seemed to be nothing holding back the winds that threatened to sweep away anything not securely anchored.

Once more Natalie had to stop and seek shelter beside one of the huge tree trunks that dotted the campus. The winds were showing no mercy as they continued to throw chunks of snow and dead leaves in her path. She shuddered, wrapped her scarf around her, and trudged along wondering what lay in store for her. She was regularly the first one to arrive at the office on any given day. Quite often she was also the last to leave.

"I love this job," she told herself. "Matter of fact, I'm not just good at it, I'm great at it."

Reminding herself that this was the reason why she kept fighting off the ever-consuming feeling of disillusionment that had become a regular addition to her day. However, no matter how hard she fought, the feelings were so overwhelming she often wondered if she had strength enough to continue.

Not only were job related issues starting to take its toll, but things in her personal life were far from ideal. With each passing day, the struggle seemed to intensify as she fought to maintain a sense of balance. She kept on fighting, desperate to keep things from spiraling out of control.

She shivered as she entered the office. It felt no warmer inside than it did outside. She placed her pocket book and briefcase on her desk, placed her lunch in the small refrigerator, and then set about turning on the heaters. These were the old-fashioned dilapidated types that only worked sporadically. At the lowest portion was a knob that required manual turning to get it started. Quite often this knob was stuck, which meant that additional manpower was always required to get it moving.

"These belong in the Smithsonian," Natalie said to herself as she fought to turn the knob.

As she busied herself with the radiators, she wondered why it always seemed impossible for the administration to find a better location for the office of the Infection Control Department. After all, this department was such a vital part of the organization; one would think that the location of the office should be easily accessible. One would expect the room to be spacious, bright, and inviting at the very least. Some nice artwork and decent carpeting would certainly help the appearance.

In fact, the opposite was true. Not only was it cramped, dusty, and poorly lit, but it was also located at the end of a long corridor on the first floor of the oldest section of the building. No wonder everyone always complained of getting lost trying to find the Infection Control office.

"If it was not against hospital safety policy, I would bring in a space heater and allow the staff to bring theirs also," she mumbled to herself. However, she knew she would not run the risk, because as head of one of the most important departments in the hospital, everyone looked to her to set a good example. As it was, the nurses brought in their own blankets, and there were times when they had to put on their coats and gloves in the office to stay warm.

Whenever the temperature outside dropped below freezing, the air seeping in around the air conditioning units felt even colder than it was outside. It was no better in the summer when the hot air seeped around the units, while constantly blowing cold air directly at the nurse whose desk sat directly across from it. It was no small wonder the staff constantly complained about one illness after the other.

Her thoughts drifted to the plush carpeting and more than adequate heating in the office of Chief Nurse Executive Samantha Brown. Samantha did not have to come into a cold office. No sir! Her executive secretary arrived in time to get the heat going and the coffee brewing before Samantha arrived.

Sometimes life is just not fair!

Natalie did not hate Samantha, but she could not help harboring a deep resentment toward her for literally taking away the job that she considered hers. After all, she had had her eyes on that position since she started working at Justice over ten years ago. She had patiently waited for Lorraine Peters, the previous nurse executive, to retire, and then she had planned to step into that position. Before she knew it, Samantha had waltzed right in and taken over, even before the position had been posted.

Talk about knowing the right people and being in the right place at the right time!

"I've done a lot for this organization. I've kept the surgical wound infection rates low. I've provided education for each and every department. I've made sure that the environment is safer than when I first arrived, and this is how they repay me. If it's the last thing I do," she mumbled, "I'll make sure Samantha Brown regrets the day she stole my job."

Natalie roused herself from her dark thoughts, returned to her office, and started preparing herself for the day. First, she checked her email and responded to the ones she thought needed immediate attention, deleted the ones in which she had no interest, and then started on her committee reports.

Despite her best efforts, she could not focus on the job at hand, and she again started thinking about the conditions in the office. She had gotten so tired of always apologizing to visitors. It was no small wonder she had developed a multitude of medical problems since assuming this position. Not only did she have to deal with the unfairness and stress related to the job, now her family life was falling apart.

"I need to take a walk to clear my head," she said to herself.

She sighed deeply as she walked to the outer office. She could feel the throbbing start in her right temple. She knew what would happen next, but she decided to ignore it. *No one must ever know about this*, she thought to herself. *I am strong, I can handle this.*

The sight of the outer office did nothing to improve her disposition. The impression of all who entered the office was of a place where one was sent to be punished for committing some unforgivable sin. The color of the walls was a drab gray, the blinds were dusty and falling apart, and the carpet looked as if it had not seen a vacuum, much less a shampoo, since the day it was installed. Whether one wanted to admit it or not, it was just a dark, depressing space.

Taking one more look around, she thought to herself, *This is how I feel inside—dark and depressing—but I'll get through this. I will. I don't have a choice.*

Continuing into the outer foyer, to her right was a small room where three nurses managed to huddle behind three small desks. In these close quarters the term 'personal space' just did not exist. The potential for transmission of infectious agents was incredibly high, and at any given time the presence of the common cold or anything transmissible was quite easily shared.

Natalie did not have enough staff to tell the nurses to stay home when they were ill. In fact, she was constantly understaffed, and it often boggled her mind at the amount and quality of work that they generated. Of course, everyone demanded and expected so much from the small and understaffed department. There were times when she had no choice but to encourage the staff to report to work, despite the fact they were not feeling well.

Thank God for a great staff. It takes a special kind of person to work in infection control, but most of all it takes dedication to work in surroundings such as these. Sometimes it feels like the most thankless job there is, but in the end, nothing feels better than saving a life. She shook her head in an effort to refocus.

Because the job consisted of an inordinate amount of documentation, both via the computer as well as hard copies, there was always a backlog. The department was responsible for generating both agenda and minutes for various committees, educational presentations, and reports for the city and state. In addition, all surveillance data, reports from environmental rounds, and all related worksheets were always required. There was never a moment to spare. Natalie rationalized to herself that if the staff reported for work while feeling ill, they could always remain in the office. By so doing, they could attempt to put a dent in their required paperwork and not visit the floors and expose patients and other employees to their illness.

Continuing along the outer corridor, not far from the secretary's desk, were two desks for the other infection control nurses, or ICNs as they were called. Also enclosed in this small area was a water cooler, a large file cabinet, and a small table where the staff would congregate to celebrate special occasions such as Infection Control Day, birthdays, and holidays.

A calm, organized environment tends to create productivity. As true as this statement might be, these strong, determined individuals proved that there are exceptions to every rule. This was easily evidenced by the vast amount of information generated from this small, dismal space and disseminated to a multitude of departments within the medical center. In addition, there were mandatory monthly reports that had to be sent to the Centers for Disease Control, the New York State Department, the corporation headquarters, and any other legitimate organization that requested infection control data.

Natalie Sinclair

Looking at the clock, Natalie realized she would have to postpone her walk until later. She had three meetings scheduled for the day, but the most pressing was the one with Samantha Brown that was scheduled for eight o'clock. She gritted her teeth at the thought of sitting in front of Samantha and smiling as if everything was okay, when deep down she knew that was not the case. She wished she could cancel, but she knew how important it was to the department for her to be there.

At a quarter to eight, Natalie started preparing for her meeting. Her business suit fitted just right, showing off her curves in all the right places. Her short blond hair was cut into a nice pageboy style that framed her face beautifully, and her makeup was so exquisitely applied it appeared as if a professional had worked her magic.

At fifty-two, Natalie looked extraordinary for her age. A strong facial feature had always been her nose, and as she looked in the mirror and applied a touch of face powder to wipe away the shine, she thought about the way she had left things with her husband on her way to work.

Despite her medical problems, her face showed no sign of aging. With the time she invested at the gym and with her vigilance about her diet, her weight was definitely appropriate for her height and frame. She never went on a "diet" like mere mortals; her genes took care of ensuring that most everything she ate burned off at a rapid rate.

As she looked in the mirror, she thought about the path her life had taken. Born of an African American father and a Caucasian mother, she had grown up in one of the poorer sections of Chicago's south side. She had acquired the fair skin and strong facial features from her mother and next to nothing from her father. She remembered the constant teasing and bullying by her dark-skinned playmates because she looked nothing like they did. Her siblings' skin tones were all darker than hers, the texture of her hair was different, and this resulted in constant fights between them. At home, she always felt like she did not belong.

She had had almost no problems academically in high school, and had received several scholarships at graduation. After finishing high school, she had attended Columbia University in New York City. She swore she would lose herself in the big city of New York and never return to Chicago. Were it not for those scholarships, her parents would not have been able to afford a prestigious school like Columbia.

She enjoyed college immensely, and felt she fitted in. She had finally found her niche. Her classmates were extremely nice, with great senses of humor, and they saw her as just another bright, driven student like themselves. She never talked much about her parents and family and rarely returned home to visit. She had no close black friends, and constantly lived in fear that someone would find out that she was not white.

Natalie had long decided to choose nursing as a career, and she excelled in all her classes. Soon after graduating from nursing school at the top of her class, she took a job at a small hospital near the university. She enjoyed working on the pediatric floor, but her chances of getting a promotion were slim to none. Because of the size of the hospital, everyone seemed to know each other including each other's families. They all went to the same birthday parties, visited the same parks with their kids, and even used the same babysitters. She felt very out of place among this small group of mothers. However, she told herself that she would only stay on just long enough to gain some experience, then she would move on to bigger and better things.

Natalie had big plans for herself, and after two years, she resigned as a staff nurse and accepted a position as head nurse in the pediatric intensive care unit (PICU) at Justice Medical Center. It was poles apart from where she previously worked. She enjoyed the large campus, the different specialties that the hospital boasted, and most of all it was a teaching hospital, which meant that there were young medical residents available. What made it even better, in her opinion, was that the majority of these residents were male. "Maybe I'll find myself a husband here," she had mused.

Natalie fitted into her new position easily, and the staff was helpful and friendly. After working in the pediatric ICU for five years, she decided that she wanted a different experience. When a position for an infection control nurse was posted, she submitted her résumé and was easily selected for the position. She enjoyed the experience of collecting data, monitoring infections, doing surveillance, educating staff about the spread of infection, and most of all she did not have to work on weekends or holidays.

It was a very different experience from what she was used to, but she enjoyed her new position immensely. She quickly developed a good rapport with the staff and the physicians with whom she worked. After five years in the department, the director resigned suddenly due to health issues and the position became vacant. Although Natalie was not the most senior in the department, she was good at her job and she wanted the new position. She did not want to appear too eager, so she decided to reluctantly broach the subject to one of her co-workers.

Catching Candace at a private moment, she cautiously asked, "Candace, do you have any interest in the director's position?"

Candace gave her a questioning look followed by a laugh. "I have absolutely no interest in that position. I can certainly do without that kind of headache. Are you interested?"

"I might be," replied Natalie, shrugging her shoulders.

Candace smiled at Natalie. "Then go for it. The girls and I were discussing it earlier and none of us has any interest in the position. We would all prefer working with someone we already know. Bringing someone new into the department sometimes creates too much conflict, so you have our blessing."

Natalie submitted her résumé and within a week, she was informed of the date for the interview. Even though she worked in the department, she knew she would have to "sell herself" to get the position. She knew the job. There was no question about it. She also had an excellent working rapport with all the physicians and nurses. There were no questions relating to areas of her job, such as resistant organisms, sterilization, or educational presentations, with which she was uncomfortable. It was the administrative part of the job of which she was unsure.

"I've taken the first step by submitting my resume, and I'm not about to turn back now," she told herself.

One great thing about infection control was the availability of answers to most infection-related questions and/or situations. All that was needed was the time and patience to diligently search for them and that was exactly what Natalie did. Even though there was scarcely any spare time in the department, she made the time. Soon she was perusing manuals, policies, Internet references, and any other resources she could find to prepare for her interview.

It was finally the day for the interview, and she arrived in the office earlier than usual. She was mildly anxious, but she knew that was not a bad sign.

"Better to be mildly anxious than overly confident," she told herself.

The interview was scheduled for nine o'clock, which suited her just fine, as it gave her time to relax and get herself together. At five minutes before nine, she presented herself at the office of Ms. Carlyle, the administrator for the department. She knew that Dr. Corbin, the infection control committee chair, would also be there. She was not disappointed, as they were both ready and waiting for her.

"Hi, Natalie. Please have a seat." They welcomed her into the office, and got the small talk out of the way.

"Well, Natalie," Ms. Carlyle began. "We asked you here because it's the policy that we interview the person for the position of director of infection control. Both Dr. Corbin and I know there is no one better qualified or suited for this position than you. We have seen your work, and we both know that you would make an excellent director. So unless there are questions that you would like to ask Dr. Corbin or myself, the position is yours."

Natalie could hardly believe her ears. She opened her mouth, but the words would not come. Finally her voice returned.

She smiled as she blurted out nervously, "Well, thank you both. I will do my best not to disappoint. I can't think of a single question right now, but I'm sure I'll have tons when I get back to the office."

"Not even about your new salary?" asked Ms. Carlyle with a smile.

"Oh yes, that."

"You'll receive a formal letter in a few days officially stating your new position and salary. I hope you'll be more than happy, but you deserve it. So you can return and start organizing your new office," replied Ms. Carlyle.

Natalie almost stumbled out of the office. If anyone had asked her later, she could not recall how she made it back to the Infection Control Department. It was all a blur.

The rest of the day passed in a daze. The staff was excited that she had been selected for the position, and promised to assist her any way they could.

"You deserve it, Nat. I know you'll do a good job," Candace congratulated her.

They had all hugged her and wished her the best.

She was happy for the appointment and felt, at long last, her plans and dreams were starting to fall into place. She loved the new responsibility, but from what she had previously observed, she was painfully aware that politics would play a large part in her new role. However, she was determined not to let it get in the way of doing what was best for her patients. Somehow she always managed to find a way around it and followed the policies to the letter.

Candace Roberts

Natalie was about to leave for her meeting when the door opened and in came Candace. It was obvious from her body language that the weather had not changed for the better since Natalie first arrived. The effects from the cold and wind were quite visible as she struggled to make herself understood.

"Good morning, Natalie," she said, teeth chattering and lips trembling so hard, she could barely get the words out.

"Hi, Candace. How are you? Did you have any problems driving in the snow?"

"No problems," Candace replied. "There was hardly any traffic. I guess most people decided to stay home today. The snow plows came through very early and cleared the roads, but this cold I can definitely live without."

Claudine, the secretary for the department had not yet arrived, and Natalie did not have time to check the messages.

"Candace, can you please check the messages until Claudine gets here? There seem to be quite a few. I hope nothing crazy happened on the weekend," she said thoughtfully. "I don't think so though, because no one called me at home. Anyway, I have a meeting with Samantha, so please page me if I'm needed." She turned and headed out to her meeting.

"Okay," replied Candace.

• • •

Candace Roberts was Natalie's right-hand person. She was dependable, knowledgeable, a hard worker and was well respected by all. She was a born leader and had often demonstrated her ability of leading the department whenever Natalie was absent for job-related purposes. Candace also had a great disposition, which was important for working in such a small department. She was the senior infection control nurse, and had been an ICN for ten of her almost forty years as a registered nurse. She had immigrated to the United States from the small Caribbean island of Antigua immediately after graduating from nursing school.

On days like these, when the thermometer dipped so low, Candace often wished for the balmy breezes of Antigua. She removed her coat, gloves, scarf, and made herself comfortable at her desk. The first sip of hot steaming coffee sent the caffeine circulating through her body, and soon she felt her body slowly begin to thaw.

Whether it was the cold or just a sudden bout of homesickness, she became reflective. Sitting at her desk with her eyes closed, she murmured to herself.

"I remember when I first came to New York and saw my first snowflake. That was such a major deal. The flakes were so beautiful; I felt like crying. I remember I was on my way to my first job interview. It was so cold, and I felt so homesick." She paused as memories and emotions threatened to drown her.

"But I knew I had to find a way to adjust, not just to the cold, but to everything. After all, I'm an optimist." She smiled at the memory.

• • •

When Candace had first arrived in New York, the sights had almost overwhelmed her. She was born and raised in a small town not far from St. John's, Antigua's capital, but had always thought of herself as a country girl. No one had been more surprised than she when the travel bug bit. So she had decided to leave her comfort zone and see what New York had to offer.

Was she ever in for a surprise!

New York was so far removed from St. John's. She immediately went into culture shock. Everything was so much larger, brighter, noisier, and busier than the island. However, never one to succumb to a challenge, she had embraced the newness and stepped out in faith, believing that she could overcome just about anything.

"Well, no one forced me into coming here. It was totally my decision. So I refuse to waste time feeling sorry for myself. I will embrace this new experience, and I'm not about to let anything get me down," she remembered telling herself.

Even though she had completed a full, three-year nursing program in Antigua and had graduated at the top of her class, she was not allowed to work as an RN in the United States.

"You have to fulfill certain requirements before you can be granted a license to work as an RN in New York," she was told.

"You can always work as a patient care aide. The money is not really that bad, and it will only be temporary," her friend Simone had told her.

"I guess I can do that," she had replied, trying hard to cover her disappointment.

Candace took this as a challenge. In order to earn money for her everyday needs, she had to put her pride aside, and accept a job at Justice Medical as a patient care aide. Her duties included delivering direct patient care, which consisted of bathing, feeding, assisting with ambulation, and the overall helping of patients. Gone were the days when she could administer medications, lead a patient care conference, or assist doctors on their rounds.

She had vowed to herself, "No matter what it takes, I will never stop until I get my New York RN license."

So she maintained a good disposition, did her job to the best of her ability, and always kept her focus. She studied as she had never studied before, and within a year she was ready to take her nursing board exams. She was very confident that she would pass with flying colors, and when the exam results were posted, she was not disappointed. She had proudly gone to the Human Resources Department, presented her license, completed the required forms, and transferred her status to a registered nurse.

Infection Control Office

As the morning progressed, the rest of staff arrived. Lisa arrived first. She was from the Philippines, and had been working at Justice for over ten years. She had immigrated to the United States with a group of her classmates and had adjusted quite well to the American way of life. The recruiting process was quite prevalent at that time due to a severe nursing shortage in the States, and many hospitals had gone to other countries to recruit nurses. A large group had been recruited directly to work at Justice Medical Center, and despite fulfilling their requirement of working three years for the facility, they had all chosen to remain.

In the beginning, they had all lived as a group in the nurses' residence, but as they became assimilated with the culture, some had chosen to expand their wings. Some had moved out of the residence and rented apartments close to the medical center, while others had chosen to continue living in the nurses' residence. As a rule, they were mostly quiet, pleasant, and nice to be around. Lisa had a kind heart and was always dependable to help in an emergency without question.

"Good morning," she sang out as she struggled to open the door leading into the office suite. As usual, her arms were overflowing with Filipino food, so Candace held open the door for her. She was well known for her tasty cuisine, as well as her high spirits, and everyone looked forward to her famous Filipino chicken and shrimp noodles. In fact, no one stayed hungry when Lisa was around.

"Good morning, Lisa," Candace responded.

Directly behind Lisa came Velma, also from the Philippines. In direct contrast to Lisa, Velma was not always pleasant to be around. Her hot temper was well known to all, so her friends were few. She had made it clear, and on more than one occasion, that she did not "suffer fools lightly." She had what one would describe as "a very short fuse," so everyone tried to stay out of her way. Quite often, her attitude made for much tension in the office.

Who could forget the time when she had completely lost control and started throwing furniture around the office? What had brought on this tantrum? Natalie had merely asked her about an incident on one of the units for which she was responsible. The incident had occurred six months prior, but it seemed like only yesterday.

As was the policy, the bacteriology lab had called regarding a cluster of Methicillin-resistant *Staphylococcus Aureus* (MRSA) wound infections. Natalie happened to be the only one present in the office, so she answered the phone and accepted the report. At the end of the day, as was the practice, everyone had gathered in the office putting last-minute touches on projects and looking forward to heading home. Wanting to make sure that this cluster was not the start of an outbreak, but also thinking that Velma might have picked up the report, Natalie casually brought up the subject.

"Velma, there seem to be a cluster of MRSA on unit two west. Are you aware?"

"No," came Velma's tart reply. "No one informed me. Am I a mind reader now?"

"No one is saying that you are. I'm asking if you're aware," replied Natalie patiently.

Taking everyone by surprise, Velma started shouting, "Why are you always picking on me. I do my share of work around here, but nothing I do is ever good enough." With that, she grabbed one of the office chairs and threw it against the door. The chair skittered off and almost landed on Claudine's head. Before getting the chance to get another weapon, Candace and Lisa, who were in close proximity, managed to get hold of her and wrestled her to the ground.

To say that everyone was in a state of shock would be putting it mildly. Natalie most of all was torn about the whole incident, and debated whether or not to report the matter to human resources or give Velma another chance. She had decided to give Velma a stern warning and placed her on notice that another incident would not be tolerated.

"Velma, you need to develop some self-control and act like a professional. I will not tolerate this type of behavior again. This is your last warning."

That was a day no one would forget in a hurry.

• • •

Solange was quiet and reserved and the newest and youngest member of the staff. She had come to the department only four weeks earlier and was still adjusting to the new service. However, she had been on staff in the medical ICU for over five years, so she was no stranger to the facility, or to some of the other ICNs.

"Good morning everyone," she said softly.

Luckily for Solange, she still lived on campus, so getting to the office was a quick jog rather than a long wait in the freezing cold at the bus stop.

"Hi, Solange. How was your weekend?" asked Lisa.

"Not bad. I went to see a movie with my roommate."

Lisa was her mentor and she really tried hard to make Solange feel as comfortable as possible.

"What movie did you see?" continued Lisa.

Solange smiled as she recalled how much she had enjoyed herself.

"You might not believe this, but we saw *Dirty Dancing*, and I really enjoyed it."

She got a dirty look from Velma, which she chose to ignore. It was her life, so who cared what Velma thought.

"I know it's an old movie, but I had never seen it before, and this theatre had a one-time showing." Her eyes shone as she continued talking. This was so unlike Solange, and everyone was happy to see her feeling so free and liberated.

"I really, really love Patrick Swayze. He's my favorite actor, so I really had a good time. I was so sad when he passed," she continued.

Velma could no longer hold her tongue, and she was tired of being ignored.

"Why do you even bother Solange? There were so many other great movies you could have seen. Patrick Swayze?" she rolled her eyes in disgust and blew a raspberry. Solange was left with no choice but to defend herself.

Her gaze locked on Velma as she advanced toward her. "Your opinions are not welcome Velma, and I do not have to ask your permission concerning my private life."

Lisa could hardly believe her ears.

"Okay, Solange. Good for you! It's time you started standing up for yourself," said Lisa.

She started smiling and clapping. Candace joined in clapping, happy that Solange had taken a stand at last. The atmosphere became heated, and angry looks were exchanged. Momentum started to build as two opposing wills were about to collide. Everyone had seen this coming, but no one knew it would come this soon.

With fire in her eyes, hands raised, and fingers pointing, Velma advanced towards Solange.

"Solange, you had better…" She didn't get a chance to complete her sentence. The office door opened, and Kirsten made her grand entrance.

Kirsten Madden 5

Kirsten floated into the office, deliberately choosing to ignore the palpable tension. However, that was Kirsten. As far as she was concerned, if it was not all about her, then it just did not exist.

"Hi, everyone. How was your weekend? Mine was fabulous."

Not waiting for a response, she quickly continued, "I had the time of my life on Saturday night." She gushed, "Everyone knows Charlie, right? He's that gorgeous second-year resident working in pediatrics that I've been seeing for a while now. I definitely think that he's 'the one.'"

All eyes rolled toward the ceiling; this was not the first time Kirsten had thought she had found "Mr. Right."

• • •

Kirsten was Caucasian, born and raised in the Bronx. She had attended Catholic schools from elementary all the way through nursing school. After joining the Infection Control Department, she had made it known that she intended to marry a doctor and no one else would do. Her reputation for flirting with any male wearing a white coat and a stethoscope was very well known. Sadly for her, this had led to more than a few disappointments along the way. Who could forget when she had rushed into the office all flushed from embarrassment and angrily announced: "Guess what everybody? I just wasted my time talking to this guy from environmental services. He was so good looking. I thought he was a resident. He had the nerve to ask me out on a date, and I was just about to say yes," Kirsten sighed.

"Then what happened?" Lisa had asked.

"Rachel from the operating room came by and asked if he had finished preparing the room for the next case. That's when it dawned on me. Imagine my embarrassment," she continued.

"So what happened next?" Lisa had asked.

"Well, I just got out of there as fast as I could."

Everyone had burst out laughing, which did nothing to help Kirsten's hurt feelings.

"Well," continued Kirsten, "I really thought he was a resident." She pouted, "I don't know why employees refuse to follow hospital policy. Talk about wasting my time." It had taken the rest of the day for her to get over her hurt feelings.

• • •

On this particular morning, Kirsten's makeup was flawless as usual. Everyone knew that if it were not for her makeup, Kirsten would be just another face in the crowd. However, she was an expert at applying makeup; it transformed her into a striking beauty. She knew that the little "genie in the bottle," as she referred to her makeup, never failed to do the trick. She knew she looked good, and she believed that no male in his right mind would ever give her just a cursory glance. With this face, she demanded a second look.

"How much time did you spend on your makeup today, Kirsten?" Candace asked with a sly grin.

"Not much time today. Only an hour," responded Kirsten. She had a wonderful disposition, however, and did not mind the good-natured ribbing from her co-workers.

Determined to continue reliving her weekend date, she continued, "Does everyone know that nice building along Carlton Highway? I always wondered what it was used for. Well, it's an entertainment hall! They had a great band on Saturday night. The food was great, and the wine was to die for. Charlie and I kicked up our heels all night, and then we went back to his place, danced, and drank some more. One thing led to another, and next thing I knew, the weekend was over and it was time to go home. So if I'm a bit hung over today, please try and understand."

She finally ran out of steam, giving Candace a chance to comment, "So it seems like you had a really nice weekend?"

"Yes, I did, and we're going out again soon," she said, barely able to contain her excitement.

"We're happy for you, Kirsten. I really hope he is 'the one,'" said Lisa smiling.

The conversation would have continued, except that Rochelle came hurrying in all frazzled and appearing as if she had ran all the way from home. It was already a quarter after nine and Natalie had not yet returned from her meeting. With this realization, Rochelle slowed her pace, sat at her desk, and got ready to discuss her weekend. No sooner than she had made herself comfortable, Natalie walked into the office.

"Rochelle, can I speak with you please?"

From her tone, everyone knew Natalie had seen Rochelle arriving late and was far from pleased. Rochelle took a deep breath, rolled her eyes, and headed into Natalie's office.

"Please have a seat," said Natalie, closing the door to her office. "What time are you supposed to be at work, Rochelle?"

"Eight o'clock," replied Rochelle.

"And what time is it now?"

"9:20."

"Did you call the office to say you would be late?"

"No. There was a lot of traffic. However, I thought I would've made it on time, so I didn't bother calling."

"That is not an excuse," Natalie replied. "This is not the first time you've been late and refused to call in. You know the policy. Don't forget, Rochelle, it's almost time for your annual evaluation. Don't be surprised when you see it mentioned."

"Okay, Natalie. Are you finished?"

"Yes, I am."

With that, Rochelle returned to her desk and prepared to start her day.

Everyone knew that even though Rochelle was dependable as far as completing her assignments, she was far from reliable where time was concerned. Everyone had wondered how long it would be before Natalie intervened. Although she had been in the States longer than most of the others, she still held on to the Jamaican "no problem man, I am on island time" mentality. To her mind, it did not matter that she no longer lived on the island where everything and everyone was still "laid back." "As long as the work gets done, that's all that matters," was her motto.

Infection Control Office 6

The Infection Control office was closed on weekends. The policy of the department was that all callers leave a voicemail. If an infection control issue occurred that could not be resolved by the nursing staff, then Natalie would be consulted by the nursing supervisor on duty. All IC nurses were issued hospital pagers, so they could be reached while on and off duty. The pagers were also necessary in order to be located in a hospital as large as Justice, because the hospital overhead paging system could not be heard in all areas.

One of the daily duties of the secretary was to listen to all messages as soon as she arrived. She would then give the messages to the ICN responsible for that particular area. The ICN would respond to the message and take whatever actions were necessary. It was the responsibility of each ICN to keep the director informed of all infection control matters occurring on their respective units. By doing so, she would have an overall picture of the number of patients on isolation, the number of patients carrying the same organism, and which patients could be safely placed together or cohorted in the same room.

Being unfamiliar with "all things infection control" was not an excuse, and the staff did not begrudge Natalie the huge responsibility it took to run the department. In fact, everyone did their best to make her look her best. Being taken by surprise on any issue relevant to the department was not acceptable.

This was the rule and everyone strove to abide by it.

A bulk of messages was always present on Monday mornings. Not surprisingly, this Monday morning was no different. While Natalie was at her meeting, it had taken Candace a very long time listening to all the messages, and transcribing them into a notebook.

As soon as Natalie had returned, she had immediately called for a meeting with the staff. She was still unaware of the information that Candace had gathered. Judging from the look on her face, Candace knew that the meeting with Samantha had not gone well. In addition, her meeting with Rochelle had done nothing to improve her disposition.

• • •

Natalie got on well with her staff and was respected by them. She often stayed calm during unusual incidents, but was known to lose her temper whenever anyone wanted her to break the rules. Because of this, she was not regarded as a team player or one of the "good old boys."

She was fuming when she had left Samantha's office.

"How dare her tell me how to run my department? When did she become an infection control nurse?" she had asked herself angrily as soon as she had left the meeting.

Although the meeting had been scheduled to address the upcoming Joint Commission on Accreditation of Hospitals Organization (JCAHO) survey, Samantha had received information about a young patient that had died over the weekend.

"Natalie, do you have any further information on the young man that died over the weekend?" Samantha had asked.

"I'm not aware of a patient dying. Why should I be aware? Did he have something infectious or contagious?"

"Natalie," Samantha almost shouted, "don't you know what's going on in your own department?"

Natalie bit back a sharp reply, took a deep breath, and responded, "Samantha, with all due respect, I didn't receive a page or a phone call the entire weekend. If there's an issue, I suggest that you, as the CNE, inform your nursing supervisors to contact me, as stated in our policy. I won't be accused of something I'm unaware of. I'll get the information and update you as soon as I know what it is you're talking about."

With that, Natalie had gathered her papers and abruptly left the meeting. She had hurriedly found a restroom, made sure she was not being observed, and threw her papers on the floor. She thought her chest was about to explode. She could barely catch her breath and started hyperventilating.

"I'm having a heart attack," she said to herself. That one consistent thought kept running through her head over and over again. She managed to stay in the bathroom stall and will herself to calm down before finally exiting the restroom and heading for her office.

And whom did she see heading in the same direction but Rochelle.

"Has anyone heard from Claudine?" Natalie asked on entering her office.

"She called to say she was not feeling well, and she was taking the day off to see her doctor," Candace responded.

"That's just what I need today," Natalie mumbled under her breath.

Infection Control Office 7

The nurses gathered around the small table as Natalie handed out an attendance sheet and an agenda. She also passed out copies of the infection control portion of the IC standards and quickly launched into her meeting.

"This is going to be the first of many meetings relating to the upcoming survey. Most of you have been through this process before, so this is really just a review. Please make sure that all surveillance data have been entered into the computer and that your hard copies are organized and accurately filed in the appropriate binder. All environmental rounds must be dated and corrective actions must be addressed. Make sure all IC policies are current and signed by the appropriate department heads. Also, make sure that at our meeting with JCAHO, we are indeed practicing what we have stated in our policies."

"Who will be present when we meet with the surveyors, Natalie?" asked Lisa.

"As far as I know, in addition to us, there will be representation from Pharmacy, Environmental Services, and Bacteriology. Of course, the Infection Control Committee director will be there, the directors of medical and surgical ICUs, the medical director, and the chief nurse executive."

This would be the first JCAHO inspection for Solange, and the anxiety was starting to get to her. She could barely get the words out as she asked quietly, "Will we be asked to speak?" She bit her lips nervously while waiting for Natalie's reply.

"Yes, we will, but we'll give you a pass this time, Solange," said Natalie with a smile.

"However, I want you to pay close attention, because at the next survey, I want you to be ready to speak. I don't want you to worry. There's still a lot for you to learn yet."

Solange breathed deeply and allowed her shoulders to relax.

Looking at the other ICNs, Natalie continued, "Be prepared to speak on your surveillance activities, isolation procedures, education, and all other activities. Rochelle, you are responsible for the neonatal ICU. Please make sure your blood stream infection rates are within the guidelines set for the unit."

"They are, except for that episode last October."

"Do you have the investigation and corrective actions documented?" asked Natalie.

"I think so," replied Rochelle.

"Don't think, Rochelle. Please make sure," said Natalie.

"Kirsten, you're following surgical site infections. How are the rates?"

Kirsten started as if awakened from a dream.

"Kirsten, are you still with us?" asked Natalie with laughter in her voice.

Startled out of her reverie, Kirsten shuffled her papers until she found the one she needed. Uproarious laughter erupted from everyone around the table.

"Yes, Natalie. I'm sorry," she blurted. "Last quarter there were three wound infections related to colon surgery. I have a meeting scheduled on Wednesday with Dr. Garcia, chief of surgery."

"Okay," replied Natalie. "Please make sure you have the appropriate documentation, including corrective actions. I need to meet with Candace, so we'll adjourn here, and we'll meet weekly until the survey starts. Candace, please stay."

With that, everyone left the table for their various assignments.

"Now Candace, was their anything special or unusual in the messages left over the weekend?" Natalie asked.

"There was a message from the head nurse on ward five south. A male patient was admitted late Friday complaining of severe abdominal pain, nausea, elevated temperature, and diarrhea. Because of the diarrhea, he was placed in a single room, but no isolation precautions were actually instituted. No isolation sign was posted on the door leading into the room, no isolation cart was placed outside the door, and no dedicated equipment was used."

"How old was this patient?" Natalie asked.

"He was twenty-five years old and a resident of a nursing home."

"He was a bit young for a nursing home, wasn't he?" Natalie said, looking questioningly at Candace.

"True," she replied, "but he had some chronic medical problems which required long term care."

The ringing of Natalie's phone interrupted any further discussion.

"Hello..." Natalie said, picking up the phone. Before she had a chance to identify herself, a strong male voice interrupted angrily.

"What is the matter with you? How dare you walk out before we finished our conversation this morning?"

Realizing it was her husband, she quietly responded, "Can you please hold?" She realized she had no choice but to take the call, so she called out to Candace.

"Candace, I really need to take this call, but we'll try and meet again later. Is there anything else that I need to know this minute?"

"Well, nothing that can't wait. There are no bacteriology results available yet, but as soon as I know, I'll let you know. The nurses have all seen the report book, so they know what to do."

"Okay, the ICU is your area. Please check and let me know what's going on as soon as possible," said Natalie. She quietly closed the door to her office and slowly picked up the phone.

"Hello…"

• • •

"Well, I guess I have to make my rounds sooner than I had planned," Candace said to herself. She started gathering all the necessary documents she would need in order to collect the relevant information. Just then, the phone rang.

"This is a busy place today, and the day isn't even half way through," she said to herself.

"Hello. Infection Control Department. Candace Roberts. How can I help you?"

"Hi, Candace. This is Francis Malloy from the bacteriology lab."

"Hi, Francis. How are you?" Candace asked.

"Well, I could be better, but no point in complaining," said Francis with a sigh. "Anyway, I have the culture results of the patient who died over the weekend."

"The name is Edwin Gonzalez, medical record # 123456. His blood and wound cultures are growing gram positive rods and they look resistant to all antibiotics."

"When will the results become final?" Candace asked.

"Well, I am working short staffed today, so I can't make any promises," replied Francis.

"In addition," she continued, "the blood cultures from the other four patients in the SICU also show similar preliminary findings."

"Okay, thank you Francis," Candace replied getting ready to hang up the phone.

Francis quickly added, "Don't hang up. I have some other results."

"Go ahead," said Candace resignedly. It was a long while before she finally hung the phone up.

Her neck was so stiff from holding the phone to her ear, she felt as if she would never regain full feeling in it again. As she headed toward Natalie's office, she tried moving her head and shoulders to work out the knot and loosen up the muscles. She was determined to let Natalie have the bacteriology results before she went on her rounds, but before she reached her office, she heard Natalie's phone ringing. Candace sighed and made an about face back to her own office.

Natalie picked up after the third ring. "Infection Control. Natalie Sinclair. How may I help you?"

"This is Brandon Saunders. How are you, Nat?"

Before she had a chance to respond, he went on, "What's this I hear about our patients dying because of a resistant bug? I hear this bug has spread to other patients. Is this true?"

Natalie took a deep breath before responding. "My nurses are investigating the situation, and I'll let you know what's going on as soon as I have all the information."

"Please get back to me soon." Not waiting for a response, he hung up. Natalie sighed, took another deep breath, and went back to her computer.

Brandon Saunders

Brandon Saunders was the hospital administrator for the facility. He had been in this position for the past five years. Despite some struggles, he had managed to keep the facility in the black. Beds were 99 percent full most of the time, which was joy to any administrator's ears.

Brandon was in a very reflective mood today. As he sat in his office, all his achievements at Justice Medical started coming back to him. To be honest, it was a very impressive list. But, this was exactly why he was being paid such a significant salary.

"Everyone knows that empty beds do not generate income," Brandon said to himself. "So a hospital filled to capacity is the only way to go."

The facility had passed the last JCAHO survey process with commendations, and another survey was due shortly. To date, there were no outstanding lawsuits, and after much battling with the unions, all employees had recently received significant raises, and everyone seemed to be satisfied.

"I deserve some peace and quiet, with no drama," he told himself, as he relaxed in his comfortable oversized office chair. Brandon was an ambitious man. "Ambition is a good thing," his mother had often told him while growing up. "Patience is a virtue," was another of her favorite sayings. His mother had been a virtual storehouse of these cute little sayings. He had loved and admired her tremendously, as she had struggled single-handedly to provide him with everything he needed. His father's only contribution toward the family was giving life to Brandon. As far back as Brandon could remember, he had never seen his father go to work. He could remember asking his mother: "Mom, why doesn't Dad go to work like other fathers?"

His mother would always reply, "Son, jobs are hard to find, but he'll find one soon. Don't you worry."

He could remember seeing his dad lying on the living room couch, and the only time he moved was when he needed to use the bathroom or to go to place his bets with his bookie. He was even too lazy to eat at the kitchen table with Brandon and his mom, so his mom always brought him his meals on a tray.

"I swear to you," his dad would always say, "my lucky day is just around the corner. Just you wait and see."

Of course, that lucky day never came. Brandon had always hated his father, and with good reason. As soon as he could afford it, he took his mother and left, making sure his father had no way of finding them.

Looking back, Brandon thought about his mother as it was approaching the fifth anniversary of her death. At various times, some of her cute sayings would come to his mind, and he struggled hard to keep them close to his heart. His had not been a happy or easy childhood, but he was a survivor. If his current situation was any indication of fighting to stay alive, then he was surely the greatest role model. He finally understood what some of her sayings meant. He agreed with most of them, all except one: "Patience is a virtue."

"I'm getting tired of waiting," he said to himself while pacing distractedly. "My patience is running out. Something had better happen soon. Real soon."

On the surface, Brandon appeared to be a team player, but patience had never been his strongest attribute. He was nice to all the right people, made all the popular decisions, and moved in all the right circles. But deep down, he had much loftier goals in mind for himself.

Claustrophobia threatened to drown him as he sat waiting to hear from Natalie. He cracked open a window and breathed a deep lungful of cold, fresh air. It did nothing to calm the tension he was feeling. He felt like a caged animal as it began prowling—his thoughts ran rampant.

"I'm stagnating. I'm fifty-five years old, and I've worked my tail off for this organization for the past five years. What more can I do to prove my allegiance to this organization? I'm Brandon Saunders, and it's time for me to move on up to the big leagues. I want to play with the big boys and call the shots. Soon I'll be Chair of the most powerful health care organization in the city, and nothing or no one is going to stop me. It's time I put my plans in motion."

He hurriedly sat down, realizing he had spoken his thoughts aloud. Luckily, his secretary Laura was off for the day, so there should be no one close by to hear him, or so he hoped. By this time, he was perspiring profusely, in spite of the frigid temperature outside. He quickly wiped his face using his expensive pocket square. He suddenly noticed that the outer door was ajar, so he quickly jumped to his feet again and quietly opened the door and peeked out to see if anyone was lurking. Seeing no one, he quietly closed the door, took a deep breath, and sat back down.

"I have to be more careful," he said quietly. "I can't let them know my plans, or someone will steal them." He smiled to himself as he became more agitated.

"After all, who would have thought that little Brandon from the projects would one day be in charge of an eight hundred-bed trauma center."

"I did all of this," he continued. "When I got here, there was nothing more than a small dilapidated, one-story building. I have fought for this, and I expect to get paid."

His face now contorted, his voice rising, he got to his feet and continued. "Now we have a twelve-bed burn unit, a birthing center, a level three neonatal unit, and a fifteen-bed medical and surgical intensive care unit, in addition to several other specialties, some of which are not even available in other hospitals in the county."

As his disorientation escalated, so did his verbal diatribe.

"If there is an outbreak of anything contagious occurring in this hospital, I want to be on top of it. No one is about to cause me my job. No one!"

By this time, all self-control had practically deserted him. However, before he toppled off the edge, he quickly opened his desk drawer and searched frantically for the only thing he knew could hold him. As his fingers located the small vial, he grasped it like a drowning man, quickly unscrewed the top, removed two small pills, and quickly drank them down with a glass of water. He slowly sat back down, waiting for the medicine to start working its magic. But before his thoughts started to regroup, he went on another tirade.

"If word gets out that there is a problem at Justice, the first thing that the 'suits from downtown' will want from me is a bunch of papers."

"Documentation, documentation," he said in a singsong voice. "I hate that word. Documentation always leads to trouble. Documentation means a paper trail, and paper trails always return to cause problems."

Slowly the medicine started taking effect, and his normal demeanor gradually returned. He quickly got to his feet, looked in the mirror, straightened his tie, and with a smile, opened his office door, and said, "I think I'd better pay a visit the SICU."

So focused was he on reaching the SICU, he never saw the outline of the figure lurking in the shadows with a cell phone turned to record.

Candace Roberts

Candace hurriedly put on her lab coat, attached her ID, gathered her papers, and headed out the door toward the SICU. As she rounded a corner deep in thought, she literally ran into Brandon Saunders. She held on to him to maintain her balance and prevent herself from falling. The close contact pleased Brandon immensely, but deeply embarrassed Candace. After dislodging herself and offering an apology, she started on her way.

Leaning his head to one side, Brandon in his most seductive voice said, "Ms. Roberts are you going to walk away without apologizing?"

Knowing his history of flirting with any female, Candice looked him in the eyes and replied, "I offered an apology, Mr. Saunders. I'm sorry if you didn't hear."

Holding her head high, she quickly walked away. She could feel his eyes boring into her back, but she dared not turn to look. She knew that would only encourage him, and encouraging him was the last thing she wanted to do.

• • •

Brandon was short in stature with a slight paunch and a squint for which he wore corrective lenses. The only attractive quality he had going was a full head of straight, jet-black hair. One could not help but admire his beautiful head of hair. It was thick, dark, and full, and it shone with a healthy glow. Everyone knew it was his pride and joy. It was rumored that he spent as much time looking in the mirror as any female spent applying her makeup.

Brandon made it easy for those wishing to have an easy laugh behind his back, and there were no lack of ridicule at his expense. One of the ongoing favorite jokes was that he was part-owner of the Clairol Corporation.

Because of his vanity, he refused to wear his corrective glasses and always wore dark glasses, even when he was indoors. His skin was very fair—the type that did not tan—and would easily burn from the slightest exposure to the sun. Every summer, he walked around with peeling skin.

People would shake their heads and say, "I guess Mr. Saunders was trying to get a tan again."

He was not a handsome man, but he certainly believed he was God's gift to women. No female was exempt from his roving eyes, and his penchant for ogling any female that happened to look his way had earned him the name "Mr. Ogle." Of course, no one would dare call him that to his face. Brandon had never married. He often told himself that soon, when he was head of the organization, he would find the right woman—a beautiful woman who would be his wife, bear his children, and help him to achieve his highest ambition.

• • •

Candace had not gone far before she heard him turning on the charm to a young nurse who happened to walk by.

As the nurse approached him, he looked at her with concern. "Excuse me, Nurse. Did you hurt yourself?"

Unfortunately for her, she was fairly new to Justice and had not yet heard of Brandon Saunders. She looked at him questioningly, wondering what he meant. Not giving her a chance to ask, Brandon smiled, knowing he had gotten her attention.

"What I meant was, did you hurt yourself when you fell from heaven? You look like a beautiful angel that just fell from heaven."

Realizing he was trying to flirt with her, the young nurse hurried on her way, embarrassed at being flirted with by someone old enough to be her father.

Candace Roberts 10

Feeling somewhat flustered, Candace continued toward the SICU, hoping her ID card would open the door to the unit. Despite the fact that this was the newest wing of the hospital, the door leading to the unit could be very temperamental. It would occasionally open if the magnetic strip chose to work as it should, but at other times there was just no budging. Whenever this happened, the only option was to call on your patience reserve. Locating and pushing a button and waiting to be buzzed in by one of the SICU staff was the only other option. Depending on the activity within the unit, the waiting time could vary sometimes from one to as high as five minutes.

Luckily this was one of the mornings when the magnetic strip worked. Candace was happy to get away from Mr. Ogle, but she was not looking forward to what she knew awaited her in the SICU. As she entered the unit, she immediately noticed that all twelve beds were occupied. The usual SICU noises of beeping respirators, IV pumps, suction machines, and cardiac monitors bombarded her senses.

The unit was very spacious, but it never failed to amaze all who entered how congested it always seemed. This was not due to a lack of organizational skills on the part of the staff; it was the name of the game in an ICU. This was what was required in order to save lives! Staff did not have the luxury of running in search of a specialized piece of equipment when a patient was coding or having a heart attack. It was best if located at a spot that was easily accessible!

The unit consisted of single rooms, and Candace's heart skipped a beat as she noticed that four of the twelve patients had green signs on the door of their rooms. Two other rooms had hot pink signs on their doors.

A green sign meant that the patient was on Contact Precautions. It was an indication that there was the presence of a resistant organism in that patient's system, and forgetting to wash your hands was tantamount to manslaughter.

A hot pink sign meant that the patient had a respiratory infection such as pulmonary tuberculosis or chickenpox, which are generally spread by the airborne route. The Airborne Precaution sign was a reminder that whenever that patient coughed or sneezed, the potential for transmitting that disease existed.

Humans are not sterile beings. At any given time, hosts of organisms are generally present on the skin and in the internal organs. Given the right environmental conditions, these organisms can develop resistance to certain antibiotics, resulting in severe illnesses and sometimes death.

A major portion of infection control is education. Educating staff on the importance of performing good hand washing is of major importance. Not only is hand washing important *before* each patient contact, it is just as important *after* each patient contact.

When a patient is on contact isolation precautions, the entire area around the patient can be infectious. Therefore hand washing is *necessary* if there is any contact with an inanimate object such as a bedside table, a bedrail, or anything within the immediate patient vicinity.

Failure to practice good infection control can result in transfer of organisms from one patient to the next. All it takes for an exposure or an outbreak to occur is a break in one single link in the chain of infection, and the result can be devastating.

An entire hospital outbreak is the worst nightmare for any facility to encounter. Not only are patients' lives at risk, but employees, visitors, and all who enter the facility are at risk.

• • •

When Candace had left work on Friday, there were no patients on isolation in the unit.

Staring grimly at all the pink and green signs, she couldn't help but wonder what had transpired over the weekend.

"I guess there's only one way to find out," she said to herself.

Candace headed for the office of the head nurse of the SICU, only to find the door closed. As she lifted her hand to knock, Carla, the charge nurse, intercepted her.

"If you're looking for Lily, she's at a meeting," she said while trying to side step Candace.

"I'm in charge," she said. "but I also have an assignment caring for two patients. I would really love to help, but sorry, I'm very busy." The nurse hurried on her way, leaving Candace staring after her.

Candace had learned a long time ago that in order to do her work well, she needed to develop a good rapport with all unit staff, but especially critical care nurses. It was a well-known fact that critical care nurses are very knowledgeable and very vocal, and they can make your life a living hell if treated less than professionally.

Deep down Candace understood that Carla was right, but she also needed to get the correct information in order to get her work done.

"I know the patient always comes first," Candace said to herself, "so I guess I'll just have to find another way to get what I need. Far be it from me to stand in the way of a patient's care."

She headed off around the corner toward the doctors' on-call room. Eddie, the Physician's Assistant who had worked the weekend had not yet left, so she cornered him just as he was about to leave.

"Eddie, what happened? Did you have to go searching for patients to fill all the beds?" she asked jokingly. They all respected Candace, and were a bit in awe of her, so a friendly ribbing at times was all part of helping to lessen the tension.

"I didn't think Infection Control had enough to do. I was just trying to be helpful," he replied with a smile.

"Try not to be so helpful next time," replied Candace sarcastically. "So tell me what happened. I notice the ICU is glowing with isolation signs. There was no one on isolation when I left on Friday."

"Well," replied Eddie smiling, "it simply means you need to be here a few weekends."

Candace gave him one of her famous eye rolls and a deep sigh, so he knew comedy time was over. He then launched into the weekend activities, and by the time he was finished, Candace felt as if her ears would never stop burning.

She thanked Eddie then headed for a quiet corner to review all the information she had received. In addition, she logged onto the computer to review the records, the available lab reports, and the paper chart of all patients on the unit. This was very time consuming but absolutely necessary.

• • •

Infection control work can be hard but also very interesting, and it is definitely not for the faint of heart. However, no matter how seasoned the practitioner, the words "exposure" or "outbreak" will spark dread in the heart of any ICN, because he or she knows the amount of work involved.

It is similar to the work of a detective. It involves long hours of investigating, seeking out, fact-finding, and collecting all pieces of the puzzle. This will entail consistent, detailed tracking and recording of all incidents and tracking the movements of every patient involved leading up to the "exposure." It is a time consuming task, but the ultimate goal is to contain the spread, so accuracy of the investigation is imperative.

Based on the information she gathered, Candace created a "line listing." This was not her first exposure/outbreak, so she was quite familiar with the information needed and knew exactly where it should be placed. Using the computer, she arranged a chart resembling a spreadsheet with rows and columns. She then placed the information on each case in a single row. In each column, which represented important variables, she placed each patient's name, age, sex, medical record number, diagnosis, date and time of admission, room number, and medical history.

She allowed additional spaces to add information such as: the antibiotics the patient was receiving, radiology exams, lab results, and also a column for other comments. Her reason for this type of organization was that the completed line listing would contain all the key information on each patient, which could then be updated as necessary. It also made analyzing the data much more efficient than reviewing the individual data sheets case by case.

Candace Roberts 11

Fair or unfair, the belief of most everyone involved in health care is that critical care nurses are very knowledgeable and confident, and therefore, they are held to a higher standard. However, what Candace observed on the unit literally threw that concept out the window.

The majority of the staff tended to be compliant, but all it takes to create an environment of danger and chaos is one non-compliant staff member. In the presence of non-compliance, a situation can gather momentum, take on a life of its own, and spiral completely out of control. This is not a situation that is desired or welcomed.

From past experience, Candace knew that everyone tried to adhere to practicing good infection control measures whenever they knew she was present. It was what happened during her absence or when they thought they were unobserved that really gave her pause!

Completing her data collection, she headed out the door. However, she quickly decided to double back in order to do some discreet observation. No sooner than she had entered the SICU, her infection control senses started tingling.

This must be what it felt like when Peter Parker transformed into Spider Man, she thought to herself.

Out of the corner of her eyes she spotted a staff member exiting a room. As their eyes connected, Candace immediately knew that this was going to be a battle of wills. Not only had this employee failed to remove her soiled gloves before exiting the room, she had also not removed the gown that she wore while caring for the patient.

"Ms. Blake," she called out.

However, Ms. Blake knew the rules and realizing she had just broken them, she was determined not to face Candace's wrath. So she picked up speed and dashed toward the restroom, intent on discarding the telltale evidence. By this time, Candace was fuming, but decided not to pursue her into the restroom. She knew when to choose her battles, and this was not the time.

"I am nothing if not patient, Ms. Blake. I'll get you when you least expect it," she said to herself and continued her observations.

As Candace headed toward the other end of the unit, she was spotted by a medical resident.

"Infection Control on the floor," he sang out.

Each group or sub-group over time tends to develop its own unique way of communication. For some reason, this was the system or code used by staff in the unit to alert each other that Candace was present. When the code went out, everyone knew to be on their best behavior in adhering to infection control protocol. This resident was obviously new to the unit, but had quickly latched on to the negative behavior, or he would have known not to trifle with Candace Roberts. Candace smiled to herself before turning. Her eyes locked on to him.

"What did you just say?" Candace asked.

His smug look changed to confusion. He started to stutter as he quickly picked up on her meaning.

"I was just joking. I didn't mean anything by it," he said.

By this time, the entire unit realized something out of the norm was taking place. Anything to break the routine! A small crowd started gathering at the entrance to each room.

No one spoke. The only audible noises came from the lifesaving machines.

Candace gave the student one of her long smoldering stares. She slowly walked toward him, looked at his nametag, folded her arms, and said calmly, "Mr. Valdez, how long have you worked on this unit?"

"One week," he said cockily.

"Did you receive my orientation when you first started here?" Candace asked.

"Yes," he said.

"Well, apparently you weren't listening to what I said, or you didn't think it was important. When it comes to infection control, it's not a joking matter. We're talking about patients' lives. Don't ever take it lightly. Am I clear?"

He nodded his head like a frightened child. "Yes, Ms. Roberts. It won't happen again." He wiped the perspiration from his face and quickly took refuge in the doctors' on-call room.

"Thanks, everyone. Show's over," Candace said loudly for everyone to hear.

Everyone quietly returned to their assignments.

· · ·

The practice of breaking the rules did not apply only to the nurses and ancillary staff but also to the medical staff. All were guilty at some point. There was also no lack of those who tried getting on Candace's good side. Little did they know that where infection control was concerned, she did not play favorites. She could not afford to, because the stakes were just too high. Life was precious, and she believed she owed a huge responsibility to each patient.

On the other hand, there were those who felt they were always compliant and never ever broke the rules. This was never more obvious than when a nurse sauntered up to Candace and proudly displayed her hands.

"See, I washed my hands," she said.

Candace smiled, but did not respond. She knew such individuals meant well, but it was her job to keep reminding them as many times as it took. Adhering to one part of the rule is not good enough. It has to be an all-out effort. Hands might appear visibly clean, but that is never good enough. Germs cannot distinguish the difference between the hands of a patient or the hands of an employee. Therefore it was just as important to wash hands *before* patient contact, as it was to wash hands *after*.

Candace sighed and continued her observation.

Candace Roberts

12

In addition to discreet observation of staff practices, observation of the environment was also an important part of infection control. It is impossible to expect good infection control outcomes when the environment is not clean. Over time and with diligent practice, it does not take a lot for an ICN to quickly spot when this is not the case.

An experienced ICN can enter a room, and in less than five minutes, identify a number of infection control issues if they are present. It would be impossible for someone without this trained eagle eye to spot the same things. It was based on this experience that Candace decided to do a quick exam of each room. This practice was done to ensure that certain standards were maintained and to quickly circumvent the potential for larger problems down the road.

It was not a daily requirement, but done solely at the discretion of the ICN. Based on the increased number of patients on isolation, Candace decided it was important that all isolation carts be checked. These carts were kept at the entrance to each isolation room and contained all the supplies needed to apply before entering a room.

Based on the Occupational Safety and Health Administration (OSHA) guidelines, it was mandatory that all employees receive annual infection control training in addition to training on an as-needed basis if requested. This mandatory training included, but was not limited to, knowledge about the contents of the carts, the correct application, usage, and disposal of its contents.

The paramount reason for checking each cart was to ensure that the appropriate supplies were present in adequate amounts. Failure to have an adequately stocked cart can result in multiple uses of equipment meant only for a single use. This could ultimately result in exposure to both staff and visitors and have a definite, unfavorable outcome.

As Candace checked the carts, she mumbled to herself, "Gowns, gloves, masks, fluid shield masks, booties, and head covers. Everything seems to be in place."

She moved from room to room until she reached the room of the patient on airborne precautions. She immediately noticed that this cart did not have the appropriate mask required for this type of isolation. After washing her hands, she found a phone and placed a call to the Central Sterile Supply Department. It was their responsibility to stock and replenish these carts daily and as needed, and usually they were quite reliable.

Candace dialed the extension and waited for someone to pick up. She was just about to hang up when someone sounding hurried and flustered answered.

"Central Supplies. David Smith. How can I help?"

"Hi, David. This is Candace Roberts from Infection Control."

"Hello, Ms. Roberts. How can I help you today?" he asked.

"I'm in SICU, and I noticed that there are no N95 masks on the cart of room twelve. This patient is on airborne precautions and needs the special masks. Could you please send someone up as soon as you can? It would really be appreciated."

"Oh, sure, Ms. Roberts. I'm sorry, but a new employee stocked the carts today, and I was not able to double check them myself."

"Don't worry, David. Just take care of it as soon as you can. Thanks." Candace hung up and continued with her rounds.

The gowns on all the carts were usually of the same color but made of different material. They were located in separate drawers and clearly marked. The ones worn by staff were fluid resistant, or impervious. This meant that body fluids including blood could not easily penetrate through the gown onto skin or clothing. This was necessary to protect the staff as they constantly worked with fluids and other potentially infectious materials (OPIM).

The ones worn by visitors were not fluid resistant, as visitors were not expected to be in such close contact with highly contagious patients.

• • •

The staff at Justice received more education from the Infection Control staff than many other facilities. In fact, so much so that the private running joke among some managers and ICNs was, "so much education and so little learning."

After finally completing her rounds, Candace realized that it was time to return to the office to report to a waiting Natalie. As she headed to the door, she started feeling light-headed. She suddenly realized she had not consumed anything all day, except for a cup of coffee at breakfast. She decided she could not meet with Natalie without first having lunch. The office was quiet as she entered. She peeked into Natalie's room.

"Natalie, I have to eat before I meet with you. I'm starving," she said.

"Of course Candace, take your time." Natalie replied.

Velma and Lisa had finished eating and had gone to do rounds on their units. Kirsten was still eating at her desk, and Rochelle and Solange were busy at their computers.

"I guess I'm the only one that hasn't had lunch?" she asked.

"I guess so," replied Kirsten. "How did everything go on the unit?"

Candace shook her head. "You really don't want to know," she replied hurrying off to the kitchen. "Let me get some lunch, and then I'll fill you in."

With that, she headed off to the small kitchen, got her lunch from the small fridge and popped it in the microwave. As soon as it was ready, she retrieved it and sat down at her desk.

"Well," began Kirsten impatiently, "what happened?"

"Well, I was only able to go to the SICU. I'll have to visit the other departments later. This is going to be a long day," Candace replied with resignation.

She went on to describe her confrontation with the medical student. They all cracked up at her imitation of the student.

"You should have seen his face," Candace laughed. "I thought he was going to pass out."

They all had a good laugh, but as everyone knows, all good things must come to an end. It was time to meet with Natalie.

Candace Roberts

13

Candace wanted to make sure that every "t" was crossed, and every "i" dotted before she presented her findings to Natalie. She checked and double-checked before proceeding to the small table in the foyer. Luckily, she had done her line listing, so this made deciphering the information a lot easier. Natalie joined her at the table.

"Okay, let's see what we have here. I hope we don't have any more interruptions," Natalie started.

"As I said previously, the 'source' patient was a twenty-five-year-old male named Edwin Gonzalez." Candace began. "He was admitted on Friday evening to the emergency room from a nursing home. According to the notes from the nursing home, he began complaining of severe abdominal pain and cramping on Tuesday."

"Only twenty-five?" Natalie asked with a skeptical look on her face. "Remind me again why he's in a nursing home."

"He's a paraplegic, the result of a gunshot wound several years ago."

"When did the bloody diarrhea start?" Natalie interrupted.

"It did not start out bloody at first, but it was very foul smelling. He had a total of three to four watery stools on Tuesday, then progressed to six daily. It became bloody on Thursday night, and his temperature spiked to 102.9 °F. He was severely dehydrated as a result of the continuous diarrhea," Candace said.

"What else?" Natalie asked.

"Well," continued Candace, "he's had an indwelling urinary catheter for quite a while and has had frequent UTIs. He was being treated on admission."

"What antibiotic was he treated with?" asked Natalie.

"I think it was Ampicillin for E.coli," replied Candace shuffling her papers. "Yes, he was on Ampicillin. One gram intravenously every six hours. His urine collected in the ER shows multiple bacteria, but culture and sensitivities are still pending."

"When did he go to the OR?" Natalie asked.

"Late Friday night his condition started deteriorating. His abdomen became distended and firm, with loss of bowel sounds, and he started having difficulty breathing. He was intubated then taken to the OR. They found there was perforation of the colon with peritonitis. He was then transferred to SICU with multiple abdominal drains and barely responsive," Candace said.

Halfway through the discussion, the phone rang. Looking at the phone screen, Candace realized it was the bacteriology lab calling. With a heavy heart, she picked up the phone, identified herself, and grabbed the report book and a pen.

"Hello. Infection Control. Candace Rob..." Before she could finish saying her name, Francis Malloy interrupted.

"Candace, I have some results for you," Francis said. "I don't think you're going to like them. Anyway, here goes. All four patients in the SICU are growing resistant *Clostridium difficile* in their blood and wounds. The final cultures from the patient who died on the weekend are also growing *C. diff*. The results were just entered in the computer, but I thought I'd call and let you know."

Candace thanked her, said goodbye, and took a deep breath.

"Natalie, we have five positive blood cultures, same organism, and same biotype. These are the four patients currently in the SICU, plus the patient that died on the weekend," Candace said.

Natalie closed her eyes. "Oh God, this is not good. Not good at all."

"Candace, you need to have a meeting with the SICU staff ASAP," said Natalie. "I'll finish going through your line listing. Please stress the importance of good hand washing and remove all hand sanitizer gels from the rooms. I'll let Dr. Corbin know what's going on."

Candace took a deep breath realizing her day was far from over. She went to her computer and downloaded information on *C. diff*, then created brief handouts. She made enough copies for distribution, gathered her papers, and left the office. As she headed back to the SICU, she sighed, "I guess I'll be spending the night here."

Natalie continued reviewing the line listing and what she found was definitely not to her liking. The more she checked, the more frustrated she became.

"I guess I'd better call Dr. Corbin. She's not going to like this at all," Natalie said.

The other ICNs had already left, but Natalie realized she needed to place that call before leaving for the day. That was how it was sometimes. Infection Control had no respect for time.

"Candace," Natalie said softly, "please go on home. You've done all you can for today. We'll pick it up again tomorrow."

"Thanks, Natalie. I'll see you in the morning." Candace grabbed her coat and proceeded to dress for the elements she knew awaited her.

Natalie was at the point of calling Dr. Corbin to inform her of the problem, but no sooner than she had started dialing, her eyes caught sight of the clock. Realizing how late it was, she quickly changed her mind and hung up the phone.

"She's such a long meter. If I call her now, I'll never get off the phone. I'll send her an email instead," Natalie said to herself.

Natalie sat down and quickly sent Dr. Corbin an email briefly outlining the problem, the actions that had been taken up to that point, and closed by telling her that she would fill her in with the additional details in the morning. Another quick glance at the clock told her that she would have a fight on her hands when she got home.

"It can't be helped," she sighed as she grabbed her coat, shrugged into it, and headed out the door.

Dr. Elizabeth Corbin 14

Dr. Elizabeth Corbin was an MD with a specialty in epidemiology. She was extremely knowledgeable about infectious diseases and was an adjunct professor at a nearby medical school. Her relationship with the infection control staff was sometimes ambivalent. However, a happy medium was always reachable.

Based on the number of occupied beds within the facility, it was a requirement that an adequate amount of epidemiologists be present for consultations on infectious diseases. Of those, one was appointed by the medical director as Chairperson of the Infection Control Committee which met monthly. It was a very prestigious position, one which required input not only from the Medical Director and the Director of Infection Control, but also from other department heads with whom she would be working closely. There was never a position for Assistant Chair, so the schedule of meetings was usually set a year in advance in order to allow for adequate planning by all members. Committee members were usually Department Heads, in addition to all Infection Control staff. Maintaining patients' privacy was always a top priority, therefore admittance to meetings of non-members was usually by invitation only.

In addition to her administrative duties, Natalie's responsibility was geared toward the day-to-day running of the department. This included the nurses' assignments, staffing, and overall general nursing-related issues. Dr. Corbin, on the other hand, was responsible for patient-related issues and infectious disease consultations throughout the hospital. In addition, she ran the Infectious Disease Clinic, lectured at the nearby medical school, and wrote position papers on infectious diseases. However, in spite of having a full plate, she often tried to insert her views on nursing issues related to the ICNs. This mostly happened during Natalie's absence, and being an independent group of nurses, the ICN's did not welcome the intrusion. This often resulted in hurt feelings on both sides.

• • •

As soon as Natalie reached the office the following morning, she paged Dr. Corbin, who responded about ten minutes later. She was in a big rush as usual.

"Hello, Natalie. I'll be there as soon as I drop my son off at school. I would've been there before, but the housekeeper was late, so that makes me automatically late. But I read your email last night, and as soon as I get to my office, I'll give you a call." She ended the call, allowing Natalie to continue with her morning routine.

The phone rang at exactly eight o'clock and Dr. Corbin asked if Natalie could come to her office.

"I'll be there as soon as Candace gets in. I want her to be there, so she can give you all the details," Natalie said.

Candace came in not long after, shivering from the cold. Not giving her a chance to remove her coat, Natalie called out to her.

"Candace, Dr. Corbin is waiting for us in her office. Make sure you have all your forms and everything you need to give her a report."

Candace took a deep breath, something she seemed to be always doing lately.

"Just let me hang my coat up, Natalie, and I'll be right there," Candace said.

She quickly slipped on her lab coat, gathered her papers, and ran to catch up with Natalie.

Dr. Corbin's office was located on the fourth floor, but they decided to use the stairs rather than wait for the elevators. Candace was breathing heavily by the time she reached the third floor. She leaned against the wall in the stairwell trying desperately to catch her breath before entering the corridor leading to the office. Natalie had already exited the stairwell and not finding Candace behind her, she returned to the stairwell, wondering what had happened to her. Seeing Candace leaning against the wall, she became frightened.

"Candace, are you alright?" Natalie asked. Concern was apparent on her face and in her voice.

"I'm fine Natalie... I'm not as fit as you are," she said breathing hard. "I should have followed my instincts... and waited for the elevator... I guess I need to go to the gym."

Candace bent forward with her hands on her knees, fighting hard to catch her breath. Realizing that Candace was okay, just winded, Natalie started laughing.

"Okay, take your time. I'll let Dr. Corbin know you'll be right in." She closed the door, still smiling, and leaving Candace to catch her breath.

Candace regained her composure and entered the office shortly thereafter. Dr. Corbin was temporarily out, so her secretary told them to make themselves comfortable. Dr. Corbin had told Natalie that she had another meeting scheduled immediately after this, so on her return, she wasted no time getting down to business.

Settling comfortably at her desk, facing both Natalie and Candace, Dr. Corbin began, "Okay, Candace, tell me what's going on."

"Well good morning to you too, Dr. Corbin," said Candace brightly.

"I'm sorry Candace. I've lost my manners, but I have so much on my mind. Good morning," Dr. Corbin said.

With the atmosphere cleared, they delved right in to business. Candace handed out copies of the line listing to make it easier for them to follow along. She started with the source patient that had died on Saturday night.

"I know about him," said Dr. Corbin. "Tell me about the other four currently in the SICU."

"Okay. The first patient is Mrs. Emma Lazar, who is a fifty-year-old female. She was admitted on Thursday evening after being involved in a motor vehicle accident. She had major abdominal trauma and multiple lacerations. She went straight from the ER to the operating room, then to the SICU. In the OR they found some ruptured bowel, which was repaired along with the lacerations. She was intubated on admission to the ER," Candace said.

"In which room was she initially placed?" asked Dr. Corbin

"Room two," Candace replied.

"Which room did Mr. Gonzalez occupy while he was in the SICU?" Dr. Corbin asked.

"Room four," Candace said.

"Is she still in that room?" asked Dr. Corbin.

"Yes, she is."

"Okay, continue," Dr. Corbin said.

"Oh, by the way, she also has a history of lupus," said Candace.

"The second patient," Candace continued, "is a scheduled admission for a hernia repair. He is a twenty-five-year-old male named Sidney Davis. He was admitted on Thursday and went to the OR on Friday morning. He has a history of asthma and developed respiratory distress while in the OR, so he was brought to SICU, room three, for monitoring."

"Was he intubated on admission to the SICU?" asked Dr. Corbin.

"Yes." Candace replied.

"The third patient is a forty-two-year-old male, Carl Murphy, who sustained a right hip fracture while playing basketball. He had no significant medical history except for high blood pressure, which is well controlled with blood pressure meds. He was admitted on Saturday and went straight to the OR. His condition was stable post-op, so he was admitted to the fifth floor south, room twelve, a single room," Candace said.

"Is that the room in which Mr. Gonzalez was first placed when he was admitted?" asked Dr. Corbin.

"Yes, it is," Candace replied.

"Oh boy, I hope this is *not* what I'm thinking," Natalie said. The wheels were turning in her head.

"Why was Mr. Murphy transferred to the SICU?" asked Natalie.

"Well, on Sunday he spiked a temperature of 102.6 °F. His wound started draining purulent fluid, and he started having difficulty breathing. He was transferred to the SICU where he was intubated. They drew blood and took wound cultures. He remains in the SICU where he is currently on antibiotics, and I understand he's not doing very well," Candace said.

"Which room is he in now?" asked Natalie.

"Room four," Candace said.

"I'm starting to see a picture, but tell me more about the fourth patient," said Dr. Corbin.

"Patient number four," continued Candace, "is a thirty-eight-year-old female with diabetes. She was also admitted to five south on Friday night after her husband found her unresponsive at home."

"Seems like they were very busy on Friday," said Dr. Corbin.

"Apparently!" Natalie replied.

"She is a new diabetic," continued Candace. "Very brittle and unsure of how to handle her diabetes. Anyway, she was stabilized in the ER and then admitted to five south."

"Which room?" asked Natalie.

"Room eleven."

"What time was she transferred to SICU?" Natalie asked.

"Early Sunday morning she was found in her bed, barely responsive, so she was intubated then transferred to room five. She is on dialysis and has a port that is now infected," Candace finished.

"How long has she been on dialysis?" asked Dr. Corbin.

"Six months," said Candace.

They continued the review, making sure nothing was overlooked. They looked at time lines, patient placement, admission dates and times, and the staff assigned to each patient. After a lengthy period, Dr. Corbin quietly stated:

"It's quite obvious what has happened here. Mr. Gonzalez is our source. He's the first one diagnosed with resistant *C. diff*, and he's the only one that had some sort of connection between all the others. Candace, I want you to find out which housekeeper cleaned the room where Mr. Gonzalez was first admitted. I bet you'll find that the room wasn't properly cleaned. Let's break for now, but get back to me and let me know what you find," she said to Candace.

Candace gathered her papers and left, knowing that her job was far from over. It was only just beginning.

Lisa Mendez

Lisa Mendez not only loved her job, she loved life. She had been married in the Philippines to her husband Marcus for twelve years. They had two beautiful daughters, Sophie and Camille, ages eight and ten years old. Her husband adored her, despite running his busy dry cleaning business, which seemed to take up all his time. He enjoyed the benefits of working for himself, but he often wished he had more time to spend with his family. He was an old-fashioned man who believed that it was a husband's responsibility to care for his family, and his wife should only be responsible for staying home and caring for him and his children.

"This is how it was with my father, and this is how it should be for my wife," he often told himself.

However, things were quite different in America than in the Philippines, and this often gave him cause to worry. Lisa, however, did not mind the idea of working. In fact, she enjoyed leaving the confines of home and looked forward to seeing her co-workers daily.

She often told her husband, "This is how it is in America, Marcus. Wives and mothers often work outside the home. This is what you have to do in order to achieve the American dream."

Marcus found it extremely hard to buy into the idea. When he had first arrived from the Philippines, Lisa had left the nurses' residence and had rented her first apartment in the States. At first Marcus did not like the idea of living in such a confined space with only a thin wall dividing total strangers and themselves.

"There is no privacy," he often complained to Lisa. "I'm afraid to raise my voice, or my neighbors will hear me."

"This is how people live in the States, Marcus. Stop complaining," she would reply angrily. In his head, he heard her words, but his heart still refused to accept them.

It had taken him a long time to get used to the idea. When he finally saw it for what it was, he had reluctantly accepted it. However, he never gave up the idea of one day owning a large home in the suburbs, so that his wife would not have to go to work daily. Lisa, however, had other plans. She had quickly adopted the American ways and had no plans to be a stay-at-home wife.

• • •

On this particular day at Justice, while Candace was up to her ears with sorting out her exposure, things were not as chaotic on the other ICNs' units. As was the practice in the department, whenever one nurse was overwhelmed with a project or a situation, the others would volunteer to help with issues occurring on the other's unit. This was why the working rapport was so great in the department. This day was proving to be one of those days when Candace really needed some help. So it was like music to her ears and not very surprising when Lisa approached her.

"Candace, I realize you're tied up with this exposure. Is there anything you'd like me to help with?" Lisa asked.

"Thank you so much Lisa. Here are my worksheets," Candace said.

Candace shuffled through the papers on her desk, found the necessary papers, and handed them to Lisa.

"Please follow up on the patients in isolation. I think there's one or two with negative cultures that can be removed from isolation. With so few single rooms, I don't want to keep them occupied if they're needed for someone else. Thanks, Lisa. You're a life saver," Candace said.

The relief was obvious on Candace's face as she handed over the papers to Lisa. Even though one issue now dominated the forefront, it did not mean all other surveillance activities came to a halt. It just meant that some responsibility would temporarily be diverted until a more stable and manageable level was reached. So as Lisa logged on to her computer, reviewed and updated culture reports, and made calls to discontinue isolation, it was evident to all why this department was really the gem of the entire medical center.

As a rule, nurses often work well with each other, but when the environment is less than conducive to working comfortably, quite often they are less than civil to each other. The opposite seem to be true for the IC nurses, and in spite of their less than ideal work surroundings, a great working relationship was quite evident.

Natalie Sinclair 16

Natalie now had all the necessary information she needed to meet with both the hospital administrator and the chief nurse executive, so she had Claudine schedule a time for the meeting. Not surprisingly, they were both out to lunch. Claudine left a message with their secretaries and was surprised when her call was returned almost two hours later. What bothered Natalie more than anything was that they expected her to meet in the nurse executive's office in half an hour.

"I guess some people can enjoy two-hour lunches, while others have to work through their lunch time," she mused.

Her mind flashed back to the number of times her nurses had gone without lunch, or had to eat at their desks while working—a habit that went against all infection control teaching.

"The world is so unfair," she said angrily between clenched teeth. "I had to wait two hours for a return call, and now she summons me to appear in thirty minutes!" Her head started throbbing but she chose to ignore it.

"Kirsten, I'll be in Samantha's office," she called out as she grabbed the necessary papers and headed out the door. However, she didn't quite make it.

For a brief second she lost her vision. She suddenly felt as if she had been hit in the head with a boulder. The attack was so sudden; it left her dizzy and nauseous. Perspiration washed over her as she struggled to regain her balance. She silently prayed, "God, please don't make me lose control."

Her chest tightened as she struggled to breathe. She grabbed hold of her head to try and keep it from exploding.

My head is going to explode, she thought to herself. The pain was so intense. As she started falling, she grabbed for the doorframe to try to regain her balance, but before her hands could connect with the door, she crashed to the floor, unresponsive.

The staff was stunned, but quickly reacted and jumped into action. Rochelle was the first to reach her side.

She grabbed her shoulders and shook, all the while calling out, "Natalie. Natalie. Are you okay?"

Natalie did not respond. Solange and Kirsten, hearing the commotion, came running from their office to see what was happening. By this time, Natalie was retching and attempting to vomit. Seeing her on the floor, they immediately went into emergency mode. Kirsten started dialing 911 while Rochelle was busy trying to turn Natalie's head to the side, so she would not aspirate her vomit.

"Natalie. Natalie," Rochelle kept shaking her, trying to evoke a response.

After what seemed like an eternity, Natalie moaned, then opened her eyes. She tried focusing on her surroundings, then struggled to a sitting position. She looked around her and saw Kirsten on the phone.

"What happened? Who are you calling?" she asked somewhat disoriented.

"I'm calling 911, Nat. You passed out. You were unresponsive, and we need to get you to the emergency room." Kirsten said nervously.

"You hang that phone up right now," Natalie commanded in a tone so unlike her that everyone froze in their spots.

"Do not call anyone. I am fine. Nothing happened. I do not need to have my personal business spread around this institution," replied Natalie.

"But Natalie…" Rochelle started.

"Nothing happened. Do you understand?" she almost shouted. "What happened here stays right here. Nothing leaves this office. Is that clear? Now get back to work, all of you. I have a meeting with Samantha."

She gathered up her papers, and with her head held high, she stumbled out of the office.

Everyone looked on in shock, mouths hanging open, not clearly comprehending what was happening. The staff all fidgeted, unsure what the next step would be. Disbelief was written on their faces.

Finally, Solange asked, "What just happened?"

"Do you think she has a heart problem?" Kirsten asked.

"I don't know," replied Rochelle. "One thing I do know, she does not want it discussed here or any place else. So we had better be careful about what we say."

Not one for mincing words, Velma piped up, "So does she expect us not to even ask her how she feels? Does she think we're completely heartless?"

"Well, you heard her. 'Nothing happened.' So if that's what the boss wants, then that's what she'll get," responded Rochelle.

Natalie's meeting lasted an hour, after which time she returned to the office. The office was as quiet as the proverbial tomb, each person thinking private thoughts. Surprisingly, on her return to the office, Natalie was in her usual spirits.

"Everything okay, guys?" she asked.

"Everything's fine," responded everyone.

"How are you, Nat? Are you okay?" Candace asked.

"I'm fine. Why?" she replied, looking questioningly at them.

"Well..." Kirsten began, "considering what just happened before you left, we were concerned."

"Well, don't be. I'm just fine," Natalie said.

With that, Natalie turned, entered her office and logged onto her computer.

Kirsten Madden

17

The next day, Kirsten had a date scheduled immediately after work. She could scarcely contain her excitement waiting for the hands of the clock to reach 4:30. She had talked about nothing else all day, and her co-workers were all wondering what clever ploy she would devise in order to leave early. She had brought a change of clothes and shoes, and everything she needed in order to play her game of seduction with Charlie.

When the department was busy, no one left work on time. This was one of those unwritten rules in the department, which often made for some strong disagreement. Overtime was not something that was easily granted, as every department struggled to stay within budget. However, Kirsten had already plotted how she was going to overcome this little stumbling block.

At exactly 4:15, she made sure she had the attention of the other ICN's before starting her performance. She got to her feet, took an exaggerated bow, and in a stage whisper, she said, "Okay, ladies. Watch and learn!"

The transformation to her face was almost instantaneous. One minute she was the beautiful, fun-loving Kirsten, and the next she looked so broken and devastated. Had the staff not known her, and if a stranger had been present, her appearance would have broken even a heart made of stone. It seemed like something she had practiced in the mirror many times over. Keeping that look in place, she turned, left the office, and knocked on Natalie's door. Natalie looked up from her report.

"Natalie, may I speak with you for a minute?" she asked with a hitch in her voice. Natalie raised her head from her report, took one look at Kirsten's face, and her heart skipped a beat. Rising from her chair, she closed her office door, and pulled a chair for Kirsten. "Sure, Kirsten, Come in and sit down. What's wrong?"

"I know that things are hectic, and I hate to bother you, but my mom just called." Kirsten stuttered as she tried to speak while trying to control the tears pooling in her eyes from spilling onto her cheeks. "She's at her doctor's office and has apparently received some bad news. Her doctor just called and asked if I could come by his office to be with her?"

"Of course. Of course. Go on. Please drive carefully. I hope it's nothing serious. Call and let us know if there's anything we can do," Natalie said.

"Thanks, Natalie. I'll let you know," Kirsten barely whispered.

Kirsten was so grateful. She could not contain the tears hovering beneath her lashes. As they started streaming down her face, ruining her carefully applied mascara, she quietly left Natalie's office. Returning to her desk with a sly smile on her face, visible only to her co-workers, Kirsten gathered her belongings and left the office to get ready for her date.

"Talk about the female of the species... That was an Oscar-winning performance if ever I saw one," whispered Rochelle.

Barely able to contain their laughter, and with hands covering their mouths they quietly closed the office door.

"How can anyone stay mad at Kirsten?" asked Lisa as she laughed, barely able to keep her voice low. However, they all knew that if the circumstances were reversed, Kirsten would come through for them in a heartbeat. She would be one of the first to go out of her way to cover for them, so this current episode would go no further than the inner office.

Kirsten had been raised in the Catholic faith and already knew what she had to do to clear her conscience. She put everything aside, left to meet her Mr. Right, and planned to have an unforgettable evening.

Rochelle Simpson 18

Rochelle was responsible for infection control issues in Women and Children's Services. This included the neonatal intensive care unit (NICU), labor and delivery, newborn nursery, and the associated clinics. One of the prides of Justice was the presence of the level 3 NICU. A level 3 neonatal intensive care unit means that there is the continuous presence of specially trained personnel. These include neonatologists, neonatal nurses, respiratory therapists, and all of the equipment necessary to provide life support for as long as needed. Staffing levels are always critical for an area such as this, and an adequate ratio is usually maintained based on hospital policy and recommendations.

This was one of the quieter services in relation to infection control, but when an event occurred, one had better be prepared to take fast action.

At birth, a baby is classified as one of the following: extremely premature infants (less than 28 weeks gestation), very premature infants (28 to 32 weeks gestation), or premature infants (33 to 37 weeks gestation).

The more premature an infant, the smaller the birth weight. When these two factors are present, the risk of complications greatly increases. The majority of infants on the unit were neonates that fall into all three groups. Being born prematurely gives babies less time to develop in the womb. Therefore the most complicated medical problems come from infants born with extremely low birth weights.

It requires a special type of dedication in order to work with babies who are sometimes so small they can fit in the palm of an adult hand. Knowledge and sensitivity are also basic requirements for caring for these neonates, and Justice Medical usually requires that staff be specially trained.

Because the area of healthcare is never at a standstill and both nursing and medical techniques are constantly evolving, there is always the need for staff to remain current and updated. Therefore, continuing nursing education courses are always being provided either by the facility or through outside agencies.

Maintaining a level 3 grade NICU is no small feat, and it requires major participation by everyone involved. One important aspect is ensuring the presence of at least one resident doctor on the premises at all times. This person must be knowledgeable, capable, and available to deal with all emergencies occurring in the NICU. In addition, he or she must be certified by the hospital as being adequately trained in neonatal intensive care, including resuscitation of the newborn. The NICU chief also holds a very important position in the unit. He or she must be credentialed by the hospital to perform all specialized surgical procedures on neonates, as well as teach the other residents under his or her care.

· · ·

There had been a cluster of four blood stream infections or bacteremia on the unit over the past month, and despite an intense investigation, the cause of the problem had not been identified. The offending organism was *Staphylococcus epidermidis*, which is a gram-positive, coagulase-negative cocci. This organism or germ is a part of normal skin flora. It is an opportunistic pathogen, and is one of the leading pathogens of nosocomial, or hospital acquired infections. Those most susceptible to infection with this organism are intravenous drug users, newborns, the elderly, and those requiring use of invasive catheters, such as premature babies.

As a rule, *S. epidermidis* is not a very pathogenic bacteria, but even simple things can become complex in relation to neonates. When Rochelle made her mandatory visit to the unit after lunch, to the untrained eye, all seemed in order. A few nurses were sitting at the nurses' station talking quietly, some administered medications, and others seemed to be absorbed in computer documentation. The unit was almost dark. This calm, quiet environment was required for neonates to sleep, develop, and grow.

With her trained eye, Rochelle detected a procedure in progress. As she drew closer, she realized that an umbilical central line was being inserted into a neonate. To her amazement, Dr. Chavez, the NICU chief attending, was not performing the procedure, but a young doctor she did not recognize. Taking a closer look, she realized she had seen him before. In fact, this was his second month in the unit, but he had been placed on the night shift. At first, she thought that she was mistaken, or her eyes were deceiving her, because only the NICU attending was qualified to insert central lines, except in an emergency. On closer examination, she noticed that the young doctor inserting the catheter wore no surgical mask, cap, or surgical gown.

Heavens only knows if he washed his hands before starting this procedure, Rochelle thought to herself. *Infection is the number one killer of these neonates.*

In addition, the NICU policy required that a staff nurse be present to assist the physician with procedures of this type.

It was quite apparent that this doctor was having difficulty with the procedure; he was hunched over in very close proximity to the surgical site. The presence of a portable light source made the confined space extremely warm. As a result, perspiration that had gathered on his face started dripping onto the surgical field, as well as onto the surgical site.

So intent was he on inserting the catheter, that he was unaware of the jeopardy in which he was placing the neonate. Rochelle's trained eyes quickly took in the situation.

She looked on in disbelief! Suddenly it seemed her feet took wings as she quickly made her way to the basinet.

Not stopping to think, she screamed, "Doctor, what are you doing?"

All eyes turned toward the sound of her voice. Ms. Grant, the head nurse, ran to the basinet followed quickly by Nurse Levy, who was assigned to the baby. By then, the resident roused himself as if from a dream. He lifted his head and wiped his dripping face on his shoulder.

"I had no one to help me," he stuttered," and the baby needed a line."

Barely able to contain her anger, Rochelle turned on the resident. "Why didn't you speak to the nurses? They would've told you that the NICU chief is the only one credentialed to insert central lines? What were you thinking?"

By this time, the resident could barely contain himself. Perspiration continued to roll in rivulets down his face.

"Doctor, will you please sit. I don't want you falling," said one of the nurses offering him a chair, which he gratefully accepted.

Dr. Chavez, the NICU attending, materialized and was informed of the ongoing events. He quickly assessed the situation and relieved the resident. After ensuring that the baby was in no immediate danger, he left for his office with a humbled resident in tow.

"I think I know now where that cluster of blood stream infection originated," Rochelle said to herself.

• • •

When Rochelle had first entered the Infection Control Department, her mentor had been a very experienced infection control practitioner (ICP). She had been very thorough in her orientation and had made many important statements. However, the one that immediately came to mind was the one about to be proven true.

Rochelle remembered those words as if she had heard them only yesterday, and luckily, she had heeded them: "Always be prepared for opportunities to educate. You may never get that opportunity again."

Those words returned to Rochelle now as she planned her meeting with the nursing staff. This was one of the greatest teaching opportunities she had encountered in her years as an ICN, and she planned to use it well.

"Ms. Grant, please gather the staff for a meeting please," Rochelle said to the head nurse.

Not only was an infection control educational opportunity relevant to the nursing staff, but the same applied to employees in all departments.

Rochelle calmed herself and gathered the staff together. She made sure a majority was present for the meeting while also ensuring that there was adequate staff left to care for the neonates. She retrieved her attendance sheet, downloaded the NICU policy relating to insertion of central lines in the NICU, and proceeded to the conference room.

Making sure that she had the attention of everyone at the table, Rochelle started, "Let me start by saying that I am really upset by what we all witnessed today. This is something that never should have happened."

Taking a deep breath, she continued, "Let me start with you, Nurse Levy. This patient was assigned to you. Why did you allow the resident to attempt that procedure?"

"I wasn't aware he was doing the procedure, Ms. Simpson. I never would have allowed it." Nurse Levy was clearly upset by the incident.

"What do you mean?" Rochelle asked calmly.

"Earlier he asked if he could insert the line, and I told him he could not. I informed him that only the NICU chief inserted lines on neonates and that I had paged Dr. Chavez. I was waiting for him to arrive on the unit," Nurse Levy said.

It was evident she felt responsible for the incident, but at the same time she was also angry with the resident.

"I guess he just wanted to get his quota of lines and didn't stop to think about the infant," Nurse Levy said angrily.

"I understand," replied Rochelle, trying hard to keep her feelings in check. "However you do understand why observation is so important? The immune systems of these neonates haven't quite developed, so they're prone to any opportunistic infections that come along. This neonate will have to be watched very carefully."

"What policies do you think were broken here today?" Rochelle continued.

Ms. Bailey, another nurse, answered, "Well, there could be some complications related to the way the line was being placed."

"Please explain, Ms. Bailey," said Rochelle.

"He did not adhere to using sterile technique, he had no nurse to assist him, plus he had no authority to do that procedure," Ms. Baily said.

"Did anyone see him wash his hands before gloving?" asked Rochelle.

"No," everyone chorused.

"How do you think the situation could have been handled differently?" she asked.

By this time, everyone wanted to be heard at once. However, Rochelle wanted them to realize the gravity of the situation, and there was no time like the present to drive that message home.

"First off," said Nancy Adams, the reigning Jamaican nurse and comedian of the group—her voice the strongest of everyone's, "I believe that this resident needs to be suspended before coming back to the unit. It certainly wouldn't hurt if Dr. Chavez started a central line on him—let him feel what it's like before turning him loose on these poor babies."

The laughter came spontaneously, but the matter at hand was anything but comedic. Even though she knew she had to remain professional, Rochelle couldn't contain herself. She was so familiar with the Jamaican sing-song tone, being from Jamaica herself. She also realized that others from the island often used this accent as a way of feeling kinship without meaning to be overly familiar or insubordinate. Trying her best to regain control of the meeting, she quickly sobered.

"Ms. Adams, I'm afraid that's not the solution, but I hear you. Let's quiet down and get back to the subject at hand," continued Rochelle. "What other potential problems can we anticipate as a result of what just happened?"

"Blood stream infection," replied Mary, another nurse.

"Sepsis," said yet another.

"That's correct. It's a big responsibility caring for these neonates. These tiny babies cannot care for themselves. Their survival is totally dependent on you. The residents are still in training, so you need to let them know what might be potentially harmful to a neonate," Rochelle said.

"What about the resident? What happens to him?" Nurse Levy asked.

The question had been on Rochelle's mind, and she intended to discuss the matter with the NICU chief. "I'll be talking with Dr. Chavez about that," she replied.

There was other input and suggestions from the nurses, and soon it was time to end the meeting.

Rochelle gathered her papers and thanked Ms. Grant for taking the minutes. It was 4:30 when she reached the office, and everyone had already left. She gathered her belongings and called it a day.

Steve and Natalie

As the days went by, things were gradually getting back to normal in the office. Natalie felt better physically, and there had been no recurrence of her attack. Despite her behavior, there was a subtle undercurrent in the office, not quite obvious, but definitely not far from the surface. It seemed as if everyone was just waiting for the other shoe to drop. One could feel it in the air, even though Natalie's condition was not openly mentioned or discussed. Concerned as the staff was, no one dared ask her how she felt, if there had been any recurrences of her fainting spell, or if she had even visited a doctor.

The truth was Natalie had not told anyone about her fainting episode. Her husband Steve and the rest of the family remained totally in the dark about her condition. Even though everything appeared to be fine on the surface, deep down she was very worried.

• • •

Natalie lived in the small town of Somerset, which was located in the most northern part of the county of Winchester. On most days, the commute took no more than thirty minutes, but when it snowed or there was an accident on the highway, the same distance could increase to two or three hours.

Her husband Steve worked in the opposite direction, further north in the larger town of Kendal. It would have been ideal if they could have travelled in to work together, but because of the locations of their jobs, this was not possible.

After Steve had completed his residency and his attending training at Justice Medical, he had been offered a position on staff. Even though he had hoped to move on to another facility, he had accepted the position of assistant orthopedic surgeon and remained on staff.

Natalie was happy when Steve had accepted the new position, as it meant they would be able to continue commuting together, except on days when he had to attend late meetings. They had enjoyed the daily commute immensely, as it gave them some extra time together to discuss their work lives, the kids, and other areas of their family life.

As everyone knows, life consists of changes, and things seldom remain the same. So when Steve was offered the position of chief of orthopedic surgery at the prestigious Kendal Medical Center, the offer was too tempting to let pass.

Kendal was a privately-owned facility with twelve hundred beds. It was a modern structure with the best state-of-the-art equipment any doctor, nurse, healthcare worker, or patient could hope for. The presence of modern equipment in conjunction with knowledgeable staff ultimately translated to better and more accurate procedures, and hence better outcomes. Kendal was idyllically located on multiple acres of green lawns and rolling hills that could be seen for miles. It had all the modern amenities, and the financial benefits were more than Steve had anticipated.

When the offer was first made, he was elated and could not wait to discuss it with Natalie. She had reluctantly given him her blessing, knowing she would miss her commuting partner but at the same time realizing it would be selfish to stand in his way. And so, Steve had started his new position at Kendal.

Steve's professional fame had preceded him, so he was warmly accepted as the new orthopedic chief. In addition, he was very well respected in his field, and all who knew him liked him for his pleasant demeanor and great sense of humor. Soon the money started flowing, and both Natalie and Steve reveled in it. They were a fun couple with lots of friends of the same social standing. Sometimes when they were playing around, they would jokingly ask each other, "What's not to love?"

• • •

Steve and Natalie had met soon after Natalie started working at Justice Medical Center, and they had dated for almost two years before they married. During the time they were dating, she often daydreamed about the day she would become Mrs. Steven Stanley, and everyone who saw them together thought they were just perfect for each other. It was so obvious they were deeply in love.

When Steve had finally asked her to marry him, she had accepted his proposal without hesitation. She realized that her dreams had finally come through, and she had indeed found herself a husband at Justice Medical.

Even though she loved Steve deeply, Natalie had decided that she wanted to keep her maiden name after marriage.

"Steve, do you mind if I keep my last name after we're married?" Natalie had asked Steve one day while discussing their wedding plans.

"Why? My name isn't good enough for you?" Steve had asked with laughter in his voice.

"No. It's just that there are so many legal documents to be changed and so many people to be notified that I don't see the necessity. You know I love you. I wouldn't be marrying you if I didn't," Natalie had replied.

Steve had leaned over and kissed her. "Of course you can keep your name. I'm secure in my masculinity. I would never allow such a minor request to get in the way of our happiness. I can handle my wife keeping her last name."

So everyone who knew her before her marriage still addressed her as Natalie Sinclair.

A year after marrying Steve, they were blessed with a son they named Tristan, followed by a daughter, Nicole, two years later. They enjoyed their family life together as a couple, they moved in the right circles, made all the right friends, and things continued to go well as some marriages do. They were blessed with smart and attractive children that were both well rounded, and easily adapted to any social setting. The children excelled in high school, made the right friends, and avoided the negative situations that seemed to gravitate to the children of some of Natalie and Steve's friends.

Time flew by and before long the kids were grown and had flown the coop. Despite their two-year age difference, Nicole was placed in an accelerated class and graduated high school earlier than usual. She graduated valedictorian of her class and gave a rousing valedictory speech. Not to be outdone, Tristan followed a close second, and as expected, they both received scholarships for high achievement to prestigious colleges. Tristan was in the process of following in his father's footsteps and was away at medical school in Boston, and Nicole was blessed with an excellent singing voice and was studying at The Juilliard School to be an opera singer. Not long after the children left home, Natalie and Steve's marriage started taking a slow descent.

Steve and Natalie

Steve had been in the position of chief of orthopedic surgery at Kendal Medical Center for quite a while now, and the job was going extremely well. He had written several position papers in the fields of orthopedic surgery, and his innovative approach to hip replacements was way ahead of its time. There were times when he occasionally came home late, but he would always call Natalie to let her know, so she would not wait up for him.

Lately, however, the frequency of his lateness had gradually increased, and the times he was actually home, he seemed to be present only in body. It was obvious to Natalie that his mind was on other things. It was as if something had started getting in the way.

Trying to relax on their deck after work one evening, neither one knowing what to say to the other, Natalie finally blurted out, "Do you think this is what they call 'the empty nest syndrome'?"

"I guess it is," Steve replied. That was the extent of their conversation. He busied himself with the paper while Natalie tried in vain to read a book, but for the life of her, she just could not concentrate.

• • •

It had been almost a year since the kids had left home, and things continued to spiral downhill. Before long, they were like two ships passing in the night. As the marital lethargy continued between them, Natalie decided that something had to change. Deciding that the present situation could not go on much longer, she decided to make every effort to impress Steve and go all out to save what was left of her marriage. Arriving home early for a change, she decided that she would make an over-the-top effort to try to bring some of the magic back.

"After all," she told herself, "the kids are gone. It's time to start rediscovering each other."

So she planned all the seductive female things that she had done to win Steve and the things she had done to keep him since they had gotten married. Out came her sexiest negligee. The tapered candles were lit, and the aroma of dinner wafted throughout the house as the wine chilled to the desired temperature. The music was soft and low, and everything was in the right place awaiting Steve's arrival. She desperately wanted more than anything to rekindle the torch.

Steve arrived home on time.

At the sound of the garage door opening, Natalie headed to the kitchen. She retrieved the wine glasses and started pouring the wine. As Steve entered the kitchen, she met him at the door and handed him a glass of wine.

Completely taken by surprise, he accepted it and mumbled, "What's this?"

"Follow me. You'll see," she said seductively, leading him by the hand into the dining room.

Steve was at a loss for words as his eyes took in the scenery.

He smiled, his eyes crinkling, "I see you've been very busy."

Natalie smiled back, "Yes, I have been."

Steve barely recognized his own dining room. It seemed to have been totally transformed into something out of *Beautiful Homes* magazine.

Around the large dining table that normally seated twelve, there were now only two chairs. The table was draped with a shimmering tablecloth, the whitest Steve had ever seen. A large red candle sat directly in the center of the table with two small white candles to the right and left. Two sparkling leaded-crystal drinking glasses were to the right of each dinner plate and wine glasses on the left side. The silverware was meticulously arranged on top of white linen napkins on the right side of each plate. Next to each wine glass was a crystal rosebud vase containing a single long stemmed red rose, while all around the table were sprinkled red rose petals.

Steve's breath caught in his throat.

Yes! That was the exact response Natalie had anticipated. She did an invisible fist pump.

"Won't you have a seat?" she asked seductively while pouring a second glass of wine. Steve made himself comfortable, and as he drank, Natalie brought in the delicious meal she had prepared.

As she reached over to help herself, Steve interrupted, "Here, let me help you."

Steve smiled as he broke a small piece of bread. He buttered it and slowly fed it to Natalie. She took it slowly into her mouth, licked the butter off his fingers, chewed, and licked her lips. They lingered over the food and when the first bottle of wine was finished, they opened a second bottle. Steve stood up, pulled out Natalie's chair, and gazed into her eyes.

"We can always clear the table in the morning," he murmured.

"Of course," said Natalie, giggling like a schoolgirl. Steve smiled, and Natalie smiled back. As they headed for the stairs, no words were needed.

Samantha Brown

Samantha had only assumed the title of chief nurse executive at Justice Medical Center over the past six months.

"It pays to have friends in high places," she often told herself.

She had been a registered nurse for almost ten years at Royal Medical Center in Manhattan, and this new position had come at just the right time.

However, the new position was proving to be bit more challenging than she had anticipated, but she was determined not to disappoint her friend Lorraine. After all, Lorraine had pulled many strings to get her the job. It was not as if she always repaid her debts, but lately she had been really trying to turn over a new leaf.

Royal Medical was a large sprawling multi-service hospital with over fifteen hundred beds. It was one of the oldest and largest teaching hospitals in the United States and was considered to be one of America's best hospitals. In addition to the main structure, Royal Medical Center had several clinics located in the outlying boroughs surrounding Manhattan.

Samantha had worked at Royal Medical as a nurse for twenty years. Not only was she smart and a hard worker, she was also deeply ambitious and very, very devious. She had always known deep down that she did not want to remain a staff nurse for much longer.

Her peers and supervisors had recognized her leadership abilities, but she was an expert at allowing others to see only what she wanted them to see. After ten years as a staff nurse she was offered the position of head nurse, followed by eight years as a nursing supervisor.

Samantha had been getting anxious and dissatisfied with her job at Royal Medical when she had received a call from Lorraine Peters, her longtime friend and chief nurse executive at Justice Medical Center.

"Hi, Sam. How are you?" Lorraine asked.

"Could be better," Samantha replied.

"Any plans for Saturday?" Lorraine asked.

"Nothing I can't postpone," Samantha said.

Lorraine knew her friend quite well and was familiar with her moods, so she knew the news she had for Sam would certainly lift her spirits. Samantha could be selfish and a royal pain in the butt at times. However, she could also be a really good friend when she wanted to, just as long as it did not take the focus away from her for too long.

"Let's have lunch. Same time, same place?" Lorraine asked.

"Sounds good to me," replied Samantha.

"I have some news I think you'll like," Lorraine continued.

"I'm listening," Samantha said.

"Oh no, it'll have to wait," Lorraine responded.

"Please, Lorraine. I could use some news to cheer me up."

"Trust me. When you hear this news, you'll be glad you waited," replied Lorraine.

"Okay, I guess I'll see you on Saturday." Samantha replied. They signed off with a firm commitment to meet on Saturday.

The week had slowly dragged as Samantha looked forward to meeting with Lorraine. She could barely contain her anticipation waiting for Saturday to arrive. She had even called Lorraine on Wednesday, hoping to get a clue as to what news she had. Nevertheless, Lorraine would not budge.

"I want to see the look on your face when I tell you the news," Lorraine had said. "I know you will be happy." With that, Lorraine hung up the phone.

• • •

Finally Saturday had arrived, and Samantha was the first to arrive at their usual meeting place. It was a quaint, little restaurant called Luigi's located in upper Manhattan near 222nd Street and Fifth Avenue. They had discovered it on one of their occasional Saturday evening summer walks. It was a bit non-descript, far from sophisticated, and could be easily missed if one was in a hurry.

By comparison, to other fancy restaurants, it could easily be referred to as a "hole in the wall." However, the most wonderful mouthwatering gourmet-style pasta dishes came from that kitchen and made one forget they were not dining at a five-star restaurant. When they had first discovered it, Samantha and Lorraine had decided to keep it as their secret and so it had remained.

Samantha had ordered her favorite drink—a strawberry daiquiri—while waiting for Lorraine to arrive.

After what seemed like hours, Lorraine finally showed up. They chit-chatted for a while and caught up on the latest gossip about their old nursing school classmates. Samantha's patience was wearing thin. Unable to bear the suspense any longer, she blurted out, "Lorraine, can you please tell me what the big news is?"

"Okay, here goes. I'm leaving Justice, and I've recommended you for my position," Lorraine said.

At first Samantha thought she had not heard correctly, and Lorraine repeated herself. A million emotions played on Samantha's face as she absorbed the news.

"Finally!" Samantha had almost screamed. "My dreams are starting to take shape."

They continued their meal while talking in between bites. In all the excitement, Samantha had almost lost her appetite, but Lorraine managed to calm her down.

"You do realize that this is a big responsibility?" Lorraine asked.

"I do. I do. I can handle it. Whatever I don't know, I'll find out one way or another. I'm a quick study. You know that," Samantha said.

"I know that," Lorraine replied. "That's what has me worried."

"Don't worry about me. You know I'm a survivor," Samantha replied, smiling.

"It's not surviving that has me worried. It's what you'll do in order to survive that gives me pause," Lorraine replied with concern in her voice.

After making her decision to leave Justice, Samantha was the first person Lorraine had thought of to replace her. However, when she remembered some of the stunts that Samantha had pulled off while they were attending nursing school, and even some actions she had taken at Royal Medical, Lorraine had cause for concern. However, loyalty to her friend had won out in the end, but Lorraine still wondered if she had made the right decision. They finished their meal and finalized the deal.

"Call early on Monday morning, before nine if possible. Brandon's usually in his best mood before nine," Lorraine said.

"Who is he?" asked Samantha.

"Brandon Saunders. He's the administrator. He'll give you all the information you need, including when to report for your interview among other things. Try not to let me down Sam," begged Lorraine.

"I won't. I promise," said Samantha, sounding almost sincere. "We've known each other for too long and have been through too much together. You're my best friend. I wouldn't do anything to let you down. I'll make you proud of me, you'll see."

They hugged and started on their separate ways.

Samantha watched as Lorraine hurried off. She suddenly remembered that Lorraine had not told her what her plans were now that she had left her job at Justice.

"Lorraine," Samantha called out.

Lorraine turned, waiting while Samantha came hurrying toward her.

"In all my excitement, I forgot to ask what your plans are now that you've given up your job?" Samantha asked.

Lorraine looked at her with a pitiful smile. "I guess you were so excited about the new job, you forgot that I told you. My mother is not well, and she needs me. My sisters are both married with young kids, and I'm still single, so I'm moving in order to be with her."

"I'm so sorry. Where does she live again?" asked Samantha.

"She lives in Florida. She moved there two years ago to avoid the snow and cold of New York."

"I hope things work out," said Samantha. "When do you plan to leave?"

"Not for another month or so. I still have a lot of loose ends to tie up though, so I don't think there will be time for us to get together before I leave. But let me know how things work out. You have my number."

"Of course I will. Take care of yourself," Samantha said.

They hugged one last time, and then went their separate ways: Lorraine thinking about her mother and her upcoming move, and Samantha already seeing herself in her new position as chief nurse executive at Justice Medical.

Natalie and Steve

22

After Natalie's night of seduction, things seemed to have returned to normal, and it stayed that way for a while. She tried her best to leave work behind at the end of the day and focus on Steve and their home. Things were going quite well, or so it seemed for a while. But it was like riding a seesaw.

At times things seemed to click, and it seemed as if things were back to the way they were in the beginning. At times Steve responded with gusto, but at other times it took all he could to muster a semblance of interest. Natalie decided that she was not about to quit and tried even harder. Soon they realized that invitations from their friends were no longer coming, and Natalie felt all she had left was her work. It seemed that somewhere in their busy lives, they had become disconnected.

Things continued to spiral downward. The few times they made a half-hearted attempt to talk, it ended with neither party having very much to say. Steve started spending more time at the hospital and began coming home at odd hours. He claimed that the hospital was planning a number of orthopedic projects and as head of the department his presence was required at different times of the day. At least that was the excuse he gave.

Natalie was getting desperate, so she decided to confront him. This was the first time she had confronted him about his lateness, and she was not really sure how to approach it. As he stumbled in late on this night, Natalie was waiting. By this time, she had just about reached her boiling point.

"Where are you coming from at this time of night?" she asked angrily.

"What time? It's only midnight," he said, looking at his watch.

"Midnight..." stuttered Natalie, "it's almost two a.m."

"I told you I had a meeting. It ran longer than expected," responded Steve defensively, still looking at his watch. "My watch is broken. No wonder ..."

By this time, Natalie was standing in close proximity to Steve. Her nose detected a familiar scent, and it was certainly not the smell of a man's cologne. She knew she had not applied any perfume after her shower, but that smell was vaguely familiar. Then it suddenly dawned on her. Steve had bought the same perfume for her birthday two years ago. She had loved the smell of it and had used it daily, but that was a long time ago. She remembered feeling sorry it was finished as she threw out the empty bottle. So why was Steve smelling of perfume that was not being worn by her?

Natalie saw red. "I certainly hope she was worth it," she shouted angrily.

Turning slowly, Steve faced Natalie and with dead calm he asked, "Are you accusing me of something?"

Natalie's heartbeat escalated. She had never before heard such coldness in his voice.

"Well..." Natalie stuttered, "that's certainly not the perfume I wear."

"You better be absolutely sure before you start making accusations. Now I'm going upstairs. I'm very tired." With that, Steve grabbed his coat and headed up the stairs toward the guest bedroom.

Natalie could not believe her ears when she heard the door to the guest bedroom slam shut. Her breath caught in her throat as the tears welled in her eyes.

Of course, in all marriages, spouses often disagree, but for her and Steve it had never happened to this degree. In spite of their occasional differences, this was the first time that Steve had chosen to sleep apart from her. Feeling as though her heart was about to break, Natalie slowly made her way upstairs toward the master suite, where she spent the rest of the night tossing and turning.

It took forever for dawn to arrive. When it finally came, she slowly dragged herself out of bed, feeling as if she had been run over by a truck and wondering if she had dreamed it all. It was not a dream. Steve's side of the bed was cold and empty, and the door to the guest bedroom remained closed.

Heading for the bathroom, she took one look in the mirror and what she saw confirmed that this was far from a dream. Slowly she got into the shower. The sting of the cold water brought her fully awake, and she quickly turned the water to warm and hurriedly completed her shower. She hoped that if things went right she would be able to leave the house before Steve woke up. The last thing she needed was to have another confrontation with him.

She dressed hurriedly and started on her makeup. However, this took longer than usual as she tried desperately to camouflage the tired, drawn look on her face.

Finishing her makeup, she headed down the stairs to make coffee. Steve apparently had the same thought, as he too came hurrying into the kitchen hoping to grab some coffee without bumping into Natalie.

They both tried to avoid any close contact, which was not difficult as the kitchen was spacious enough to accommodate a large crowd. Skirting around each other, they appeared like two wrestlers warming up to go on the attack. The tension was palpable; you could cut it with a knife.

Sipping her coffee, Natalie was unable to take the silence any longer. She finally blurted out, "So what really kept you out so late last night?"

"I told you I had a meeting," Steve replied nonchalantly as he sipped his coffee.

"I don't believe you!" yelled Natalie, staring angrily at him.

"That's your problem," replied Steve with a shrug.

"If you can't get home at a decent time, maybe you should not come home at all. Apparently you're more interested in your work than in your home."

With that, she grabbed her briefcase and her car keys and headed out the door, slamming the door behind her.

Steve started after her, his anger mounting. "Natalie, are you sure that's what you want…" He never finished the sentence, because Natalie had already slammed the car door, started the engine, and was getting ready to back down the driveway.

So things kept moving downhill in increments, and Natalie started working longer hours.

"What's the point of going home to an empty house? I no longer have a marriage," she told herself.

Infection Control Office 23

When Natalie had taken the position of director of Infection Control, she had made it a policy to meet with the ICNs weekly to review infection rates and get an overall sense of what was happening throughout the hospital as it related to infections. It was generally an informal gathering, but with the emphasis on something serious about infections, and the staff all looked forward to learning something new. In this setting, they all felt at ease to ask their peers questions that they were mulling over, or just to get a sense of how one might handle a situation differently. As they gathered at the table in the main foyer, they were all in good spirits, laughing and joking good-naturedly with each other.

As they gathered at the table, Natalie opened the meeting with some general comments before calling on Candace.

"Candace, why don't you start, seeing you've been having some excitement in the SICU," Natalie began.

"Okay." Candace replied as she settled comfortably in her chair, "everyone's aware of the *C. diff* exposure which started on five south."

"Yes, Candace," Rochelle interrupted. "I think it's a very juicy case. Tell us about the source patient. It sounds quite interesting."

"Well, Mr. Gonzalez was a young male admitted from a nursing home after being treated for a UTI. He developed *C. diff*, which became so pervasive, that despite massive use of the appropriate antibiotics, he succumbed to his illness," Candace said.

"Candace, sorry to throw this on you so unexpectedly, but this is a great case. It will be a good learning experience for everyone, especially Solange. We'll use this as a sort of case discussion," Natalie interjected.

Candace sighed and made a face. "Natalie, I wish you had told me earlier. I'm not prepared."

"Oh, Candace. You're familiar with the case. I know you can do this," Natalie said.

"Okay," Candace sighed. "As everyone knows, *C. diff* are anaerobic, spore-forming rods or bacilli normally found in the intestines. When the bacteria in the colon of a normal person have been destroyed by broad-spectrum antibiotics, the gut becomes overrun with *C. diff*. This overpopulation is very harmful because the bacteria release toxins that can cause bloating, severe diarrhea, and abdominal pain, which can also become very severe. *C. diff* is the most serious cause of antibiotic-associated diarrhea and can lead to pseudomembranous colitis, which is a severe inflammation of the colon. Peritonitis, which is inflammation of the lining of the abdomen and perforation of the colon, can also occur. *C. diff* infections can also progress to toxic mega-colon, which is a marked dilation of the colon, and this can also result in death."

"Are you saying that taking antibiotics causes this problem?" asked Solange.

"Well, it usually results after taking broad-spectrum antibiotics over a long period. *C. diff* normally resides in the gut, but the spores can be accidentally ingested while individuals are patients in a hospital or a nursing home. The strain that causes major problems appears to be more virulent with the ability to produce greater quantities of toxins A and B. In addition, it's more resistant to a group of antibiotics known as floroquinolones."

Everyone sat in rapt attention as Candace wrapped up her presentation.

"Excellent presentation, Candace," Samantha interjected with a broad smile.

"That was so very informative," Solange chimed in. "I didn't realize that antibiotics can cause that many problems."

"Yes," replied Candace. "That's why they should not be prescribed unless absolutely necessary. Antibiotics will only work on bacteria, never on viruses, so they won't cure the common cold. They will, however, work on the complications of a cold, such as pneumonia if it's caused by bacteria."

"But what if your doctor orders it, shouldn't you take it?" Solange asked.

"Most doctors will never order an antibiotic based on symptoms of the common cold alone. However, you will find that some patients believe that an antibiotic is the cure for any and everything. Hopefully doctors will never allow themselves to be pressured into ordering antibiotics unnecessarily. Taking antibiotics when they're not needed is really just laying the groundwork for development of drug resistance," Candace said.

"How does drug resistance occur?" asked Solange.

"Well, antibiotic resistance usually occurs when bacterial species are able to survive exposure to one or more antibiotics. Because exposure to antibiotics is such a common phenomenon these days, pathogens have become quite smart. They have to find a means of survival, thus they have developed resistance to multiple antibiotics, and that's how the term multidrug resistance or MDR originated," Candace said.

"Thanks, Candace," replied Solange, looking in awe at Candace, wondering when she would be as knowledgeable or as confident.

"Any more questions for Candace?" asked Natalie.

"Yes. What about the four other patients who were exposed? How were they exposed, and how are they doing?" Kirsten asked.

"Well, the first patient had major abdominal surgery. She also has a history of lupus, which often leads to long-term or chronic inflammation. Because of this, she is receiving high doses of corticosteroids, an immune system suppressing drug," Candace said.

"How did she contract *C. diff*?" Kirsten asked.

"That's a very good question." Candace said. "Apparently, there must have been some cross contamination. Maybe someone forgot to wash their hands properly after caring for Mr. Gonzalez. I'm still looking for the connection."

"How old is she?" Rochelle asked.

"She's fifty-two." Candace replied.

Realizing she had their full attention, Candace continued discussing the case. It always made her feel good inside when she could help to enlighten her co-workers, especially when they were new to the area of infection control, as was the case with Solange.

"She is intubated, which has also contributed to a decrease in her immunity. She has developed pneumonia, which is being treated with antibiotics. She's the sickest of the four who were exposed," Candace said. She took a deep breath. "I hope she makes it," she said caringly.

"What about the others?" Lisa wanted to know.

"The second patient is twenty-five years old and also has a history of asthma. However, he's not intubated. His wound is healing well. His cultures are negative. He should be transferred out of SICU very soon," Candace said.

Shuffling her worksheets until she found the one she wanted, Candace continued, "It's very interesting how patient number three, Mr. Murphy, contracted his infection. He was transferred from the OR directly into the room where the source patient, Mr. Gonzalez, was first admitted."

Not wanting Solange to feel excluded, Candace turned and directed a question at her. "Can you tell us how Mr. Murphy could have gotten infected? Keep in mind that Mr. Gonzalez was already transferred to the SICU, and the room had been cleaned."

Solange reacted with a start. She could feel her body getting warmer as all eyes turned toward her. She told herself, *I'm not going to be nervous, but I don't want to appear foolish either.*

Different scenarios kept running through her head, but she was still unsure of the correct response. She finally blurted out, "I'm not sure…"

"Think about it." Candace said coaxingly.

"Well," Solange began haltingly, "maybe they forgot to clean the bed."

"No, I'm afraid that's incorrect. During my investigation, I spoke with the environmental services employee, and she assured me that the bed was thoroughly cleaned. Does anyone want to take a guess as to what happened?" asked Candace, looking from one to the other of the ICNs.

"If the bed and all the furniture in the room were thoroughly cleaned, I can't imagine how the bug was spread," said Velma.

"Would you like to take a guess, Lisa?" Candace asked.

"I can only think of one thing, but I'm not too sure," Lisa said.

"Okay, let's hear it," said Candace.

By this time everyone was feeling energized and trying their best to guess what could have caused the contamination.

"First, let me ask, what disinfectant was used to clean the room?" asked Lisa.

"Why does that make a difference?" Candace asked, hardly able to hide the look of triumph on her face.

The other ICNs suddenly realized at what Candace was aiming. It was as if a light bulb went off in everyone's heads, and they all started talking loudly. They all wanted to be heard at once as they realized where the problem had originated.

"Oh, she did not use chlorine bleach, did she?" Rochelle shouted.

"Oh, I can't believe I missed that," said Kirsten incredulously.

"That was a good one, Candace. Can you please explain why it's important for bleach to be used for cleaning *C. diff*?" Solange asked.

"Okay," Candace picked up the conversation. "*C. diff*, as you know, is a very hardy spore that can survive routine cleaning products that do not contain bleach. So all surfaces should be carefully disinfected with a one in ten diluted bleach solution."

Candace had the attention of all the ICNs, so she continued to cover as much as she could because the opportunity might not present itself again.

"Soap and warm water is a better choice for hand washing," she continued.

"Alcohol-based hand sanitizers do not destroy *C. diff* spores. Washing with soap and water allows the spores to wash off your hands and down the drain," Candace demonstrated with her hands as she spoke. "Visitors should also be diligent about washing hands with soap and warm water before and after leaving the room or using the bathroom."

"And now we come to the last patient, Ms. Fagan. She's a thirty-eight-year-old female who's a new diabetic. She was unresponsive when admitted to the ER, was stabilized there, then transferred to five south. She became unresponsive again and was transferred to SICU to be intubated.

"Did she go to the OR?" asked Solange.

"No, she did not. However, she has a hemodialysis port, which is now infected. She remains intubated, and her blood sugar is very erratic. Her blood cultures remain positive for *C. diff*. She's still spiking a fever. That's all I have for you today," Candace said.

Candace took an exaggerated bow, smiled, and took her seat.

"Excellent presentation Candace, for someone who was unprepared," said Natalie, clapping and smiling with pride. Everyone at the table joined in.

"Thank you, Natalie," Candace said.

The room cleared as the staff returned to their various assignments.

Natalie sighed. "Things are going pretty well here. I wish things were going this well at home," she said to herself.

Samantha and Brandon 24

Not long after Samantha joined the staff at Justice Medical, she quickly aligned herself with Brandon. It seemed as if they were kindred spirits who automatically gravitated toward each other. No one who knew them was surprised that an unholy alliance had been formed. They both had this singular desire to excel at all cost, and woe to anyone who got in their way. They had shared secrets relating to their personal lives, as well as their jobs, but secretly they had started wondering if they had shared too much.

They were having coffee in Samantha's office on the morning she broached the subject of the *C. diff* on SICU.

"Brandon," she said coyly, "how many patients currently have this *C. diff* bug?"

"I think there are four of them. Why do you ask?"

"How many cases have to be present for Infection Control to report it to the CDC?"

"I'm not sure. Why?" asked Brandon.

"Do you always have to report it to the downtown office?" she asked slyly.

"I'm not sure about the number, but it has to be reported," Brandon replied. A look of concern started to make its appearance on his face, as the wheels in his head started turning.

"Think about it, Brandon." Samantha said, looking thoughtfully at him. "If this is reported, you know what will happen. It won't take long for the newspapers to get hold of it and blow it out of proportion."

Brandon jumped to his feet. "I think I'm beginning to understand. I need to make sure this does not leave the walls of Justice. I have too much at stake to let that happen."

Not stopping to finish his coffee, he reached for his coat and headed for the door.

"I'll talk to you later, Sam." Brandon barely got the words out before he was out the door. Samantha grinned devilishly to herself as the door closed and Brandon headed towards the bacteriology lab.

Not bothering to wait for the elevator, he entered the stairwell, determined to reach the bacteriology lab before the reports were called in to Infection Control. He was breathing rapidly. His face reddened from the exertion of climbing five flights of stairs.

He took a deep breath to calm himself before opening the door. As he entered the lab, he was assaulted by chemical fumes, which were normally found in labs that handled human specimens.

"In the long run, all this discomfort will be well worth it," he told himself. He spotted Frances and hastily made a beeline in her direction. Surprised to see him in the lab, Francis gave a start and tried to head him off before he contaminated her specimens.

"Mr. Saunders, what brings you up here this early? I don't recall ever seeing you here. How can I help you?" she asked.

"Well Frances, I've been meaning to pay you a visit to tell you thanks for the excellent job you've been doing," Brandon said.

Frances leaned against the table, head to one side, and smiled slowly. She just could not believe her ears. She knew Brandon Saunders too well to believe a word of anything that he was saying. Anyone who knew him well knew he had an ulterior motive for almost everything he did.

"I'm serious," he continued. "I don't say this often enough, but I really appreciate all the hard work that you and your staff are doing. Take this nasty bug in the SICU, what's the name?"

"*C. diff*," replied Frances.

"Do you report to anyone else besides Infection Control?" he asked.

"Well, I have to report it to the local Department of Health depending on certain factors," she hesitated.

"What do you mean 'certain factors'?" he asked cautiously.

Sensing that his questions were more than just of a casual nature, Frances hesitated, her suspicions getting the better of her.

"Why do you need to know this, Mr. Saunders?" she asked.

"Oh, I just wanted to know how your department works. I've decided to make a special effort to get to know my employees better and to get a sense of what they do. This way, I can appreciate them even more than I already do." He smiled, but the smile did not quite reach his eyes. Realizing he would not get the information he needed, he decided to try a different tactic.

"By the way Frances, I haven't forgotten about that conference you would like to attend in Chicago next month. It's for two weeks, right?" Brandon asked.

"Yes, two weeks," replied Frances.

"It's a lot of money, but we want our employees to be up-to-date on all the new things happening out there. I have the forms all signed and ready for you. You can pick them up whenever you want to," he said.

Brandon gave Frances one of his fake smiles, and Frances, realizing what he was talking about, returned one of hers.

I'm not for sale Brandon. Two can play this game, was the thought that went through her head.

"Thank you, Brandon. I'll pick those up as soon as I get a chance," she replied.

"You're welcome, Frances. As they say, 'one hand washes the other.'" He again flashed one of his fake smiles.

Realizing he was not going to get what he wanted, Brandon turned and was about to leave when Frances called out, "Mr. Saunders, you can get all that information from Natalie. She has all the guidelines for reporting to the different agencies. I know she'll be able to give you all the information you need."

"Thank you, Francis," he said between clenched teeth as he headed out the door.

"If Natalie Sinclair was the last person on earth, I wouldn't ask her for anything. She's so straight-laced, she would die before giving me any information," Brandon said to himself angrily.

Frances slowly closed the door behind him. She was not one to be overly suspicious, but the incident just did not feel right.

"I wonder what that was all about. That's very unusual, very unusual indeed." She headed for her office, closed the door, picked up her phone and dialed.

Natalie picked up her phone on the second ring.

"Hi Natalie, this is Frances. Do you have a moment?"

"Of course, Frances. I always have time for you, you know that," Natalie said with a smile.

"I just wanted to give you a heads up. Brandon was just here asking a lot of questions."

"Questions about what?" asked Natalie

"It might be nothing, but it just seemed unusual. He wanted to know how many cases of *C. diff* there were altogether, and did we have to report them to the downtown office and to the CDC. I told him that he should ask you."

"Hmm, very interesting," replied Natalie. "I wonder what he and that Samantha are planning. I'll be ready for them, but I doubt he'll call me. Anyway, thanks for the heads up Frances."

Natalie sat thinking about what Frances had just told her. *I can't trust those two. I know that they'll do whatever they can to get their way, but I'm ready for them.*

Natalie Sinclair 25

So far winter did not seem to be abating. Getting to work each day remained a Herculean task. No place was winter more evident than in the employees' parking lot at Justice. At the sign of the first snowflake, without fail, the snowplows stopped working, and on the occasions when they did work, there seemed to be no other place for banking the snow except the top of employees' cars.

Natalie had made an appointment to see her doctor after work and anxiety had started to set in the minute she got out of bed that morning. It seemed liked the longest day of her life as she kept eyeing her desk clock. When her mind was not on her job, it was on her marriage, then back to her appointment. She was starting to find it difficult juggling all these thoughts and still functioning as efficiently as was normal for her.

Four o'clock finally came and everyone was surprised when Natalie was the first to leave the office. She gave no explanation just that she had to leave early.

"That's not like her to leave so early," Lisa commented.

"Maybe she's just trying to get home before the snow starts again," replied Candace.

Natalie struggled through the snow toward the parking lot and finally made it to her car. She started the engine and waited for it to get warm while she rubbed her hands together to generate some warmth. With her gloves on and her scarf tightly wrapped around her face and neck, she ventured out and tried removing as much snow from the windshield as she could. The temperature had dropped since this morning, so underneath the snow, there was nothing but solid ice. Natalie was able to remove just enough ice from the windshield to enable her to see for a short distance while driving.

"I guess the heater will just have to take care of the rest," she said out of sheer frustration.

As she backed out of her assigned parking space, her mind started wandering about her appointment. So deep was she in thought, she failed to notice a large black vehicle that had just pulled out of a space and parked directly behind her. She put her car in reverse and gingerly touched the gas pedal. She turned slowly to try and visualize her position. As she slowly backed out, she was just in time to see the black car pick up speed and head towards the gate of the parking lot. With her heart beating like crazy, she hit the brake pedal, and yanked open the door, ready to confront the thoughtless jerk.

"What the hell is that idiot doing?" she asked angrily.

To her dismay, she saw it was Brandon Saunders. With that close encounter, Brandon quickly turned to see who was exiting the car that almost slammed into his precious Benz. He recognized Natalie heading towards him with fire in her eyes. He knew he had two choices. Number one, stay and apologize to Natalie for almost causing an accident, or two, get the heck out of Dodge. Being the coward that he was, he chose the second option. But before he did, he turned and gave Natalie a dirty look then kept on going.

"That would have been some way to end my day, crashing into the Mercedes Benz of the hospital administrator," she said to herself.

She returned to her car and allowed time for her heart to gradually return to normal.

"I won't let this upset me. It takes more than Brandon Saunders to upset me today. I have more important things on my mind," she told herself.

• • •

Natalie made it to her doctor's office without incident, and for a change, the waiting room was not crowded. She was shown in to see the doctor almost immediately.

Dr. Macintosh had been her primary care doctor for many years and was almost like a father figure to her. He greeted her as always with a hug and a kiss.

"Natalie! Where have you been hiding yourself? I haven't seen you in quite a while," Dr. Macintosh asked.

She smiled at him, already feeling relaxed. "Dr. Mac, you always say that. It hasn't been that long since I saw you."

He inquired after her husband and the kids and then got serious.

"So what brings you here today?" he asked.

Natalie could barely get her words out. Never before had she been at a loss for words. As the tears welled up in her eyes and cascaded down her cheeks, she told him about the symptoms she had been experiencing.

"So what took you so long to get here?" he asked. Taking a deep breath, she told him about the problems she'd been having both at home and at work. As the tears continued to flow, she poured her heart out. Finally, after what seemed like hours, she sat quietly with her shoulders down, her eyes downcast, drained and spent of all emotions.

The doctor looked at her, kindness written all over his face, "That was quite a lot to keep bottled up inside. I'm sure you feel much lighter now."

Feeling better than she had in a very long time, she looked at him and smiled. "Yes I do," she replied.

"So now that you've used up all my tissues," he smiled, "let's try and find the source of these headaches."

Dr. Macintosh did his usual examination, head to toe was his habit. He was nothing if not thorough, and that's why Natalie and her family had kept him as their family doctor all these years. He did not believe in shortcuts, and he also did not believe in mincing words. After completing his exam, he returned to his office, allowing Natalie time to complete dressing.

As she took her seat by his desk, he looked up from his notes.

"Nat, from my initial exam, I can't find anything specific to make a diagnosis," Dr. Macintosh said. "I would need to order additional tests, so this is what I'm going to do. I'm going to recommend you see a neurologist. He'll know exactly what tests are needed, and this way we'll save some time in case there is anything wrong."

Natalie looked him in the eyes. "You're not hiding anything from me, are you Dr. Mac?"

He returned her look. "Natalie, I've never lied to you, and I'm not about to start now. What I'm saying to you is this. Based on the history you gave me, I want you to see someone more equipped to make a diagnosis. I'm not a neurologist, and just in case there is something going on in that brain of yours, I want you to find out sooner rather than later."

He busied himself looking for something on his desk.

"Now is there anyone you would prefer to see? Maybe someone where you work?" Dr. Macintosh asked.

"No," replied Natalie hastily. "I would prefer seeing someone away from Justice. Sometimes there is no privacy, and I'd rather keep my private life separate from my work."

"I understand that quite well. Anyway, here's a list of neurologists," he said, handing her a sheet of paper. "They're all very good. You choose who you want to see. And Natalie," he paused and looked her directly in the eyes, "please don't wait too long to make this appointment, and please let Steve know what's going on."

"I will. I promise," replied Natalie.

Dr. Macintosh gave her a fatherly hug before she started the long ride home.

As she entered the highway, she wondered what awaited her at home. She didn't have too long to wait as her cell phone started ringing. Glancing at the display, she recognized Steve's number. Her heart skipped a beat as she pushed the answer button.

Thank God for blue tooth! With the push of a button, you're connected. No need for holding the phone in one hand or against your ear and shoulders while attempting to drive. This meant you could drive safely with both hands on the wheel as required by law.

Of course, the newer cars came with blue tooth already built into the steering wheel, but for now the little attachment to the ear worked just fine.

At first blue tooth had seemed so intimidating, Natalie thought, but after it had been installed and explained by the geek at the phone store, it would have been quite difficult living without it.

"Hello, Natalie. Are you there?" Steve asked.

Rousing herself, Natalie realized she was daydreaming and that Steve was at the other end of the phone.

"Oh, hello Steve. I'm here," Natalie said.

"Where are you? Are you coming home soon?"

"Yes, I'm on my way. I should be home in about twenty minutes."

"Okay, I'll see you when you get here. Bye," Steve said.

Natalie shook her head, not sure of what she'd just heard. Steve did not sound angry at all, and for the first time in a long time, he was home early. This was most unusual! Matter of fact, he almost sounded as if he was in a good mood.

Curiosity was about to get the better of her. "I wonder what he's up to?" she asked herself as she tried to stay within the speed limit.

Natalie and Steve

26

Natalie was almost hesitant to open the door. However, she need not have worried. As she slowly opened the door and peeked in, there stood Steve with a glass of wine in hand and a smile on his face.

She was speechless. This was the last thing she expected. To say she was surprised was to put it mildly, so she just stood with her mouth opened.

"Why are you standing there? Come on in," Steve said, giving her one of his drop-dead smiles. She had really missed that smile. It had been absent for way too long. Oh how happy she was to see it again.

Natalie hesitated. "Are you sure?" she finally asked.

"Why wouldn't I be sure?"

"What about last night and this morning? Are we going to pretend it never happened? " Natalie asked, looking at him questioningly.

"I did not say that, but Nat, we've been married for too many years to let one argument end what we've had. We've invested a lot in this marriage, and we can't let it go down without a fight," Steve said.

He offered her the glass. "Here, have some wine and let's talk."

Natalie seated herself on the couch and Steve took the sofa. An uncomfortable quiet surrounded them both as each wondered where to begin. Eventually the awkwardness passed, the apologies were out of the way, and the words and feelings started to flow. They were unaware that there were so many aspects of their marriage that needed to be addressed. All the doubts and fears that were long submerged were brought to the surface. In the end, the cathartic feeling that was created seemed to bring them so much closer to each other; they wondered why they had not done this sooner.

Steve suddenly broke out laughing as he looked at Natalie.

"Why are you laughing?" asked Natalie, suddenly feeling self-conscious.

"I just realized that we could probably open our own marriage counseling business," replied Steve.

"Yeah, right," replied Natalie. "If only it were that easy."

Natalie happened to glance at her watch. She was amazed at the time. Jumping up off the couch, she cried out, "Steve, do you realize the time? I had no idea we were talking so long. What are we having for dinner?"

"Don't worry. That talk was way overdue. We shouldn't keep things bottled up like that ever again. And by the way, I ordered dinner. It should be arriving any time now," Steve said.

"Oh, that's so nice! By the way, there's one more thing I need to talk to you about," Natalie said nervously.

"I don't like the sound in your voice, Nat. What is it?" asked Steve.

"Okay, I'll get right to the point. I went to see Dr. Mac this evening." She bit her lips as she tried to figure out the best way to deliver the news.

"Well, I've been having some really bad headaches lately," she continued. "Oh, I've also had a few episodes where I passed out."

"What," Steve shouted, anxiety all over his face. "You passed out? Oh my God. How long were you planning on keeping this from me?" He got off the couch and started pacing. "Never mind. What did Dr. Mac say?"

"He recommended I see a neurologist as soon as possible."

"Okay, let me think." Steve scratched his head and rubbed his forehead as he paced. Suddenly it came to him.

"There is a really good neurologist at my job. His name is David Guthrie. He's a colleague and a friend. I'll give him a call. I'm sure he'll see you tomorrow if I ask him to," Steve said. "By the way, don't plan on going to work tomorrow. This has to be taken care of right away."

"Okay, I won't go in to work tomorrow," Natalie agreed. She smiled to herself. "I love it when he's so masterful."

Dinner arrived shortly. They picked at it absentmindedly, both worrying about how Natalie's recent news would impact the rest of their lives.

As soon as dinner was finished, Steve placed a call to David, and everything was arranged for the following morning.

Soon they headed off to bed. However, sleep did not come easily for either one. Lying there, they tossed and turned, each lost in their own private thoughts. At long last, Natalie finally fell into a deep, peaceful sleep, happy that Steve had moved back into the master suite. It was good to know she didn't have to keep secrets anymore.

Natalie and Steve

True to his word, Steve had managed to get an appointment for the following day with David Guthrie, the neurologist. He was up earlier than usual after getting very little sleep; he was so worried about Natalie. As he fixed breakfast, his mind started to wander.

"I can't afford to lose her," he sobbed.

The thought of living without her had never entered his head. Realizing that Natalie was awake and could walk into the kitchen at any time, he quickly dried his eyes and continued fixing breakfast. The last thing he wanted was for her to see him cry.

Driving to the hospital together would have been a great idea, but Natalie was stubborn and refused his suggestion that they drive together.

"How would I get back home?" she asked. "I can't sit around your office all day. I have things I need to do at home," she insisted.

"Okay, keep your cell phone within easy reach," he told her as he did a last minute check before getting into his car.

"Stop fussing, Steve. You sound like a mother hen," she smiled up at him as she adjusted her car seat.

Having lost the battle, he made sure that Natalie drove ahead of him. In case she needed him, he would be right behind her. He really would have preferred if she did not have to drive, but what she had said earlier did make sense, so he went along with it.

• • •

They lived north of the city, so it was not unusual to see more snow after a big snowstorm, and Steve expected a difficult drive ahead. As they headed for the highway, he noticed that the local streets were almost free of snow, despite the recent storm. The driveways were also free from the unsightly mounds of dirty snow that was usually so prevalent in the city, especially after the plows went through.

I guess that's why I pay those high taxes, Steve thought to himself.

Surprisingly the highway was free and clear, but Steve drove cautiously, realizing that Natalie was taking the same precautions. It seemed as if a lot of drivers had chosen to take off from work today, and who could blame them! One could not be too cautious driving in winter, especially when there was always the hidden danger of black ice.

The day was bleak with the sun hiding behind the clouds, and according to the weatherman, it was going to remain that way most of the day. Snow hung from the branches of most of the trees, creating beautiful winter wonderland scenery.

"Just like a Christmas postcard!" said Steve, trying to keep his mind occupied with anything but what lay ahead.

They made excellent driving time and reached Kendal Medical by nine o'clock. They had no problem with parking, as the hospital always did a good job of clearing the parking lot immediately after any significant snowfall. Steve led the way to Dr. Guthrie's office.

"The flowers are all gone, but the snow is so beautiful," Natalie commented, gazing out at the hills in the distance.

"Yes, they are," Steve replied absentmindedly.

Their appointment with David was for 9:30, so they had a little time to spare.

"Let's go to my office for a few minutes. We can at least leave our coats there," said Steve as the elevator climbed to the fifth floor. Both his and David's office were on the same floor, just a few doors down from each other.

Natalie nodded.

Before long, they both headed to David's office, each deep in their own thoughts. David was waiting for them and opened the door as soon as they knocked.

"Hello, David. Why are you opening your own door? Where's your secretary?" Steve asked smiling while shaking David's hands.

"She'll be coming in late today. That gives us more time to talk," he laughed.

"David, you haven't met my wife Natalie. Natalie this is David Guthrie," Steve said.

Natalie did not mean to stare, but she couldn't help herself. She was hypnotized by the most gorgeous pair of blue-grey eyes she had ever seen on an African American male. His long, thick lashes would be envied by any woman. He was at least 6'10" with a smile that reminded her of Denzel Washington's.

This is one gorgeous hunk of a man! I wonder if he has ever played basketball professionally, she thought to herself. She wanted to ask him so badly, but of course, that would be so inappropriate. Her eyes quickly wandered to his left hand. But of course, he was married! Why not? Which woman in her right mind would allow this tall drink of water to slip away? No one she knew!

Realizing she was staring, she cleared her throat nervously. "It's so nice to meet you, Dr. Guthrie. My husband has said so many nice things about you. It's nice to finally meet you."

Her entire body felt like she was on fire, and she was almost sure her face was as red as a cherry.

She removed her hands from his. She could not remember if they had actually shook hands. As Natalie sank into the deep plush fabric, she thought, *this is the most comfortable office chair on which I have ever sat. They are even more comfortable than Steve's.*

Steve had located the website the night before, and Natalie had filled out the required medical forms. They had been emailed via a secure website, and Dr. Guthrie had received them and reviewed them before they arrived.

With the introductions taken care of, they got underway.

"Natalie, I've already gone over your forms, but why don't you tell me in your own words what brought you here today," Dr. Guthrie said.

Natalie told him about the symptoms she had been experiencing. She told him when the headaches started, when they felt more intense, all the other symptoms accompanying them, and the recent episode of fainting that she had experienced. She left nothing out. He did not interrupt, giving his full attention to her every word, from beginning to end.

By the time she finished talking, she felt empty.

"Is there anything else?" asked Dr. Guthrie when she stopped talking.

"I think that's all," replied Natalie.

"Okay, what I need to do next is a thorough physical and neurological assessment. Steve, you can stay if Natalie doesn't mind," he said looking from one to the other.

"I don't mind. He can stay," Natalie replied.

From Natalie's knowledge as a nurse, she knew this was going to be very thorough, and nothing would be overlooked. In the end, Dr. Guthrie did not disappoint.

He started out by checking her vision, hearing, balance, coordination, and reflexes. He explained as he examined.

"Some of these tests might seem unnecessary, but I want to check to see if there is anything out of place, because difficulty in one or more area of your brain may provide clues about the part that could be affected by a brain tumor to any number of other things," Dr. Guthrie explained.

Natalie cooperated as best she could, and after an hour, she felt as if she had been prodded and poked in every part of her body.

"Your physical findings are non-specific. What I'll need are some X-rays, an MRI, and I'll get some blood off to the lab also. Are you free to have these done today, or do you have to hurry off?" he asked.

"No, I'm free all day," Natalie replied.

"Okay. The faster I get these orders to radiology, the faster you can be on your way. Someone will be here to take you to x-ray. You can wait here, or you can wait in Steve's office. It's up to you," Dr. Guthrie said.

He gave her another of those drop-dead smiles, and for a moment, Natalie almost forgot she had a headache.

She was shuffled first to the chemistry lab where they drew at least six vials of blood, then to the Radiology Department where they X-rayed her head, neck, and spine in a multitude of different positions.

She was starting to feel like she was in the middle of a marathon.

The next test was a magnetic resonance imaging (MRI) of the brain. Natalie was familiar with the term, the machine, and even what to expect, however, she never had a reason to actually experience one. Until now!

As she entered the room, the infection control nurse in her rose to the surface. In that role, the first order of business was to ensure that all surfaces of the machine were clean and free of any potentially infectious materials that could contaminate a patient. This could include blood, wound drainage, stool, or any type of body fluid. She breathed deeply as a quick scan told her there was no visible blood on the machine. She also noticed that everything was neat, clean and quite welcoming. However, this was never a guarantee.

She shook her head and quickly told herself that she was a guest at this facility and as such, she would do her best to act the part.

As she sat on the edge of the table, her heart sped up. She knew Steve was in the observation area, but how she wished he could have been able to come in the room with her. Knowing that was an impossible wish, she lifted the rest of her body onto the table and made herself comfortable. She knew the machine contained a very strong magnetic field, and she had made sure to remove all objects from her person that would attract the magnet.

The MRI scanner consisted of a large doughnut-shaped magnet with a tunnel in the center. As the table started sliding noisily into the tunnel, Natalie closed her eyes and tried to take some deep breaths. As a rule, she did not have a fear of confined spaces, but she could not help but think, *This must be what it feels like to be in a coffin.*

There was barely space to move her arms. Then again, the radiologist kept telling her, "Keep very still. Don't move."

Before entering the tunnel, the radiologist had explained to Natalie that the test would take about twenty to thirty minutes, and that there would be a series of varying sounds. There would be some loud knocking of varying length and intensity, along with periods of quiet. In between the noises and the quiet, there was some soft music that greatly contributed to Natalie's sense of relaxation.

Natalie held on tight to the call bell that had been given to her at the start of the test, but thankfully, there was no need for using it so far.

And soon, the test was over!

When she finally met up with Steve, she was tired and starving, and she could feel a headache starting in the left side of her head.

"I must say, he's really thorough," said Natalie as she flopped down in a chair in Steve's office. "I can't think of one test David didn't request."

"Yes. He is," smiled Steve. "By the way, I couldn't help but notice that you were bowled over when you met him this morning,"

Natalie smiled coyly. "Me? Bowled over? I have no idea what you're talking about."

She stood up, still smiling. Grabbing Steve by the hand she said, "I'm starving. Let's go eat."

Steve shrugged into his lab coat smiling as they headed out to the cafeteria.

Brandon Saunders 28

Brandon was not in the greatest mood today, and anyone who knew him could see that. He usually came to work early, but today he was in his office even earlier than usual. Today he was dressed in a dark business suit and a well-starched light blue shirt, and a dark red tie finished off his ensemble. His jet-black hair was more wavy than usual, and at first glance, one could easily mistake him for a banker, which in some ways he was like a banker.

First on his agenda, was to try getting some information from Natalie about those pesky bugs in the SICU. He only hoped he could do it without raising her suspicion.

"I think I'll just be wasting my time by talking to her, but nothing ventured, nothing gained," he told himself. If he could not get what he wanted from her, then he would have no choice but to go to the very top and ask Dr. Elizabeth Corbin. He didn't want to appear as if he was interfering, but they had left him no choice.

"After all, Liz would never have gotten that position without my recommendation,' he said to himself.

He knew that Natalie came in early, so he decided to surprise her by dropping by her office. He knew if he called, she might just make up an excuse about some meeting or other. But if he just showed up unexpectedly, she would have no choice but to see him.

"I hope she has forgotten the incident in the parking lot," he said to himself.

Heading in the direction of the Infection Control office, he was surprised at the appearance of the hallway.

"It's been a long time since I had a reason to visit this area," he said to himself, staring down the long, dark corridor.

A shudder ran through his body as he hurried down the corridor and knocked on the office door. "The faster I can get what I want, the faster I can get out of here."

As usual Natalie arrived at work early. She was anxious to make up for time lost while visiting the neurologist. She was busy poring over some statistical data when she heard a knock on the door. She decided not to respond. *Maybe they'll get fed up and leave*, she hoped. However, that was not to be. The impatient knocking continued, so she decided to get rid of whoever it was so she could get back to her work.

It's a good thing the door is always locked, she thought irritably. She hurriedly scanned her calendar. "I can't imagine who could be calling this early. I have no appointments," she said.

The interior upper half of the door consisted of frosted glass, so it was impossible for anyone to see inside the office. Unfortunately, it was also impossible to see outside.

"Who's there?" she asked hesitantly.

"It's me, Brandon," he answered impatiently.

Reluctantly she opened the door. "Oh, Brandon," she said, feigning surprise. "I can't recall seeing you before in this office. What brings you here at this early hour?"

"Well, can't I visit my favorite infection control director?" he asked, all sweet and syrupy while moving in for a hug.

Natalie managed to side step him to avoid his hug, knowing full well the nature of his fishing expedition. Deciding that two could play this game, she smiled and invited him in. She offered him some coffee and chitchatted about the weather. All the while, Natalie kept wondering when he would start talking about the real reason for his visit, as well as his behavior in the parking lot. As they chatted, his eyes kept roving around the room. *I can't imagine how anyone can work in this dump*, he thought while thinking about his well-appointed office.

Finally Brandon decided to move in for the kill.

"Natalie, I have a couple of questions, and I thought you would be the best person to ask." He hesitated as if asking Natalie's permission. She knew better, but hey, why not play along.

"Ask anything you'd like. I'll do my best to give you an answer," she replied.

"I know we've been having a problem with *C. diff*, and I was wondering how that was going?"

"It's under control," Natalie replied. "Thanks for your concern."

"I just wanted to know if the hospital is in trouble, and if there's anything I can do to help. Also are there specific agencies you report infections to, and do you need a specific number of infections before you can report them?" he asked.

Natalie pretended to be taken aback by his questions. She gave him a long questioning stare. "Brandon, before I answer your questions, I'd like to ask you one myself."

"By all means, Nat," he said, shrugging his shoulders and smiling.

"Why do you need all this information? This is not the first time we've had a cluster of infections, and you've never shown any interest before. What's so different about this time?"

You could blame Brandon Saunders for many things, but no one had ever blamed him for not thinking fast on his feet.

"Well, Natalie," he said slowly, "as you may be aware, there's a freeze on, and the budget is very tight. The last thing we need is for patients to be afraid to come to Justice Medical."

Natalie continued to play the game. She opened her eyes wide with surprise. "What do you mean, Brandon? Why would anyone be afraid to come to Justice?"

"Well, don't we have an outbreak going on? Haven't patients been dying every day? What do you call that?" he shouted. His face and neck turning a deep red while his nostrils flared dangerously.

Natalie fought hard to keep herself from smiling, but it escaped.

This was the worst thing she could have done, because it just served to enrage him more.

"How can you sit there and laugh at a time like this? Don't you realize how important this is?" he railed. "When the newspapers get a hold of this, and you and I no longer have a job, then you'll realize this is not a joke."

Natalie had never seen such a quick change in anyone's demeanor. As he rambled on, she feared he might suffer a stroke right there in her office, so she thought she would humor him. At the same time, she also wanted to get him out of her office as fast as possible.

Softly she began talking as if to a child. "Brandon, there is no problem. I have to report infections to the downtown office, but this exposure does not meet the criteria to be considered an outbreak. Don't worry. Everything will be fine. You don't have to worry."

She continued speaking softly, until he eventually calmed down.

"Are you sure, Natalie?" he asked sounding frightened.

"Yes, yes. No need to worry," she said.

He abruptly sat down and Natalie offered him a glass of water. He drank it down quickly and took a deep breath. Feeling more like his old self, he got back to his feet.

"Thanks, Nat. You have no idea how worried I was. Thanks for the good news. I'll be on my way so you can get back to work," he said.

He shook hands with Natalie and headed for the door. Before reaching the door, he turned, "Natalie, let that be our little secret, okay?" he said winking conspiratorially.

"No problem Brandon," she smiled.

Natalie closed the door behind him, grateful that he was finally gone. She felt physically drained from what she had just witnessed. Of course, she didn't have the heart to ask him about the incident in the parking lot.

"What the heck was that all about?" she asked out loud.

Dr. Elizabeth Corbin

It was now almost two months since the first case of resistant *C. diff* had been identified, and things were more or less returning to normal. As was the policy of the Infection Control Department, Dr. Corbin required a meeting to bring her up-to-date on hospital-acquired infections throughout the facility.

Bright and early this morning, Natalie and Candace were summoned to Dr. Corbin's office for a command performance. Not anxious to repeat the incident of the last time she went to her office, Candace decided to wait for the elevator. Natalie, of course, chose to walk up the five flights.

Not surprisingly, Natalie was the first to arrive, and definitely not surprising, Dr. Corbin was busy with a phone call. Candace eventually arrived, and this time, thanks to the elevator ride, her respiratory rate was just where it needed to be. Acknowledging their presence, Dr. Corbin held up a hand to indicate she would be off the phone shortly.

They both took their seats thinking the meeting should be over in ten minutes tops. Five minutes went by, then ten. The hard wooden chairs were starting to take a toll on their delicate rear ends. Both Natalie and Candace started shifting from one cheek to the next as their patience started wearing thin. As if reading each other's mind, they both rose as one, deciding to leave and reschedule the meeting.

Taking one look at them both, Dr. Corbin knew she had overdone it this time.

"Alex," she said into the phone, "could we finish this later? I have a meeting scheduled, and my staff has already been waiting for the past ten minutes. It sounds like a very interesting case, and I'll be more than happy to see the patient. Let me get back to you as soon as I finish my meeting, okay? Bye."

After apologizing profusely, Dr. Corbin focused her attention on Natalie and Candace.

"I'm so sorry guys, but I had no choice but to take that call," Dr. Corbin said. "Apparently this attending has a patient who has developed some very unusual symptoms, and he wants me to take a look at her. Anyway, Candace, let's hear what's been happening since we last met."

As usual, Candace, who was a master at organization, was ready with her report, which fortunately was far better than the last time they had met. She handed out a chart so Dr. Corbin and Natalie could follow along and then delved right in.

"The last time we met, there were four patients, so I'll start with those. Mrs. Lazar was the first patient admitted following the source, Mr. Gonzalez. She was the motor vehicle accident. Her injuries were so severe, she did not survive," Candace said.

"She also had lupus," Natalie interjected, "so her body was not able to continue fighting."

"Yes," continued Candace. "In the end she suffered multiple organ failure. Hemodialysis was able to sustain her kidney function for a brief period, but she had a severe episode of bacterial pneumonia. She also had multiple episodes of UTI and fungal blood stream infection which weakened her chances for survival."

"I can understand," said Dr. Corbin, nodding her head. "Lupus can cause major immunosuppression. Contracting resistant *C. diff* only made it easier for her to succumb."

"She survived for two weeks," Candace continued.

"I'm surprised she lasted that long," replied Dr. Corbin.

"The cultures that were obtained all grew *C. diff*, even those that were obtained in the emergency room. The biotype was also different from the source patient's, so I've classified her infection as "community acquired." It's not reportable to the CDC," Candace said.

"I agree," responded Dr. Corbin.

"Mr. Davis was much more…" Just then, the desk phone rang. Candace stopped mid-sentence.

Dr. Corbin motioned for quiet, "Sorry, my secretary is out today, but I'll get rid of whoever it is," she said picking up.

True to her word, she was able to get rid of the caller after promising to return the call as soon as possible.

"I'll let the machine take the calls from now on," she promised, returning her attention to Candace.

"Okay, where were we?" she asked.

Candace picked up where she left off. "As I was saying, Mr. Davis was much more fortunate than Ms. Lazar. He has age on his side. Although his original stool culture had grown *C. diff*, and he had developed some diarrhea, this subsided shortly and subsequent cultures were negative. He was transferred out of the SICU after two days and has been discharged home."

"The third patient, Mr. Murphy, who was placed in the same room as the source patient is now colonized. He is stable but remains in the SICU. He now has a tracheotomy, but no longer requires a ventilator to help him breathe," Candace said.

"I see he has been on some major intravenous antibiotics. Metronidazole and Vancomycin?" Dr. Corbin interjected.

"Yes, his stool and wound cultures are still positive, but his temperature has been normal for quite some time now," Candace replied.

"Unfortunately for him," Natalie said, "he ended up going to the OR for repair of a ruptured bowel."

"That's so unfortunate. This is definitely hospital-acquired," said Dr. Corbin, shaking her head. "This was a strong healthy guy. The only problem he had was high blood pressure, and now he has a trach. Let's hope he gets nothing else while he's here. Candace, please make sure that he's receiving daily physiotherapy. I think he needs to be transferred to in-house rehab. I'll discuss this with the SICU chief. Candace, please remind me."

"And the last of the four?" Dr. Corbin asked, looking at Candace.

Candace consulted her chart once again. "Ms. Fagan," began Candace, "has done surprisingly well. Her diabetes is now under control, and she's had two sets of negative blood and wound cultures."

"Is she still in the SICU?" Dr. Corbin asked.

"No," replied Candace. "She was recently transferred to a single room on one of the floors."

"I know this area is not specifically yours Candace, but do you know if she's receiving diabetic teaching?' asked Dr. Corbin.

"I'm not sure, but I can certainly find out," she replied.

"Thanks, Candace." Dr. Corbin said.

The phone had not stopped ringing since the meeting began, so Dr. Corbin was anxious to return her calls, as the majority of messages sounded as if they needed immediate attention. She stood up indicating the meeting was adjourned. Before they exited, she asked, "Are there any new cases?"

"There are some community-acquired on the floors, but so far no further cases of hospital-acquired," Candace replied.

"Keep up the good work. Thanks again. Natalie, I'll talk to you later," Dr. Corbin said. She was already dialing the phone before Candace and Natalie made it out the door.

Infection Control Office

It was now the end of February and winter was still continuing its unrelenting bite. There was currently eight feet of snow on the ground, and the weatherman had just predicted another twelve inches. Everywhere you looked there were mounds of snow. And there was nothing worse to look at than dirty, brown slushy snow. It had been days since anyone had even see the ground. As usual the office was still cold, and everyone was complaining.

"With all this snow and ice, there's no place to walk. Seems like winter keeps getting longer and longer," said Kirsten irritably. "The street is like a skating rink. I have lost count of all the people slipping, sliding, and falling." She started laughing. "This morning this elderly lady slipped and started falling. Someone tried to help her, and they both went down and started sliding down the hill on their butts. As she slid down, someone tried grabbing onto her, and that person lost his balance and started sliding. It was like an avalanche..." She could barely get the words out as everyone in the office cracked up laughing. Tears were streaming down their faces as they watched Kirsten trying to recreate the scene.

"My asthma has been acting up so badly, sometimes I just barely make it to work," fussed Claudine, after everyone had regained their breaths. "If this cold continues, I might have to take a leave of absence."

"Have you been taking your medicine?" asked Lisa concerned.

"Yes, but sometimes it makes me feel so bad, I just want to stop taking it," Claudine said with frustration.

"You can't do that. Have you told your doctor? Maybe he can prescribe a different medication," said Lisa, walking over and placing her arms tenderly on her shoulder.

Claudine started to cry. In between sobs, she tried talking. "As if I didn't feel bad enough about myself... he told me that I need to lose fifty pounds or my diabetes will never be under control. Do you know how hard it is to lose one pound, let alone ten?" she shouted. "He also wants me to stop smoking," she continued as tears flowed down her face.

Lisa listened calmly and patiently, sympathy all over her face. A few encouraging words were all Claudine needed and Lisa was adept at giving those. Finally, the tears subsided and the hiccups began.

"Thanks Lisa. It feels so good to have someone to talk to. My daughter is going through the same thing, and I can't talk to her," Claudine said.

The tears started all over again.

Just then, Velma came barging in, lips trembling from the cold. Noticing Claudine wiping her eyes, she smirked. "What's your problem? It's too early to be bawling your eyes out. Do you think you're the only one with problems?"

Lisa turned on her, "Velma, have a heart. You don't even know what the problem is, so just shut your mouth."

"Yes, Velma, stop interfering. You don't even have all the facts," said Rochelle.

Even Solange piped up, "Try and be nice for once, Velma. You might like it."

Feeling like she was being attacked, Velma yelled, "What is this, pick on Velma day? I can't get in here before everyone starts picking on me."

Everyone did a double take, and then chaos broke loose.

Rochelle jumped in first. "Excuse me. Picking on you, Velma? You're always giving your negative comments and being insensitive to everyone's feelings. How dare you talk about anyone picking on you?"

"You've got to be kidding," Candace chimed in.

"You must be out of your mind," yelled Kirsten at the top of her lungs.

Natalie entered the office amidst yelling and screaming. She thought her staff had all gone crazy. She just stood and observed, wondering how long it would take for them to realize she was there.

Candace was the first to spot her. Trying to get everyone's attention was going to prove difficult, so she quickly yelled, "Good morning, Natalie."

Immediate silence descended as all eyes turned toward the door.

Like a mother hen about to chasten her chicks, Natalie stood silently and looked from one nurse to the other. She turned and calmly asked, "Would anyone like to tell me what's going on?"

All eyes fixed on Candace.

As the senior ICP, the others expected her to go to bat for them. Not this time.

Natalie shook her head, "I didn't ask Candace. Everyone here can speak for themselves, as will Candace."

Everyone started talking at once. After multiple stops and starts, the story finally came together.

"So Velma, you've done it again?" asked Natalie, giving her a look that said, "you've really blown it this time." "Can I see you in my office please?"

Brandon Saunders 31

Brandon was a very happy camper as he left Natalie and headed to Samantha's office.

"I hope she's in early today. I can't wait to share my news." He smiled as he headed toward her office.

He knocked on her office door and pushed it open without waiting for a response to enter. Samantha gave him a look that said, "How dare you barge into my office without waiting to be invited?" However, like a chameleon, the look was gone even before Brandon was able to detect it.

As he sat, he smiled and hummed as if he did not have a care in the world.

Samantha gave him a questioning look. "What's up Brandon? You seem in such a good mood. I could use some good news for a change."

Brandon continued smiling like the cat that had just ate the mouse. "Sam, my dear, we have nothing to worry about. Like FDR said in his first inaugural address, 'We have nothing to fear but fear itself.'"

He suddenly turned serious. "I just came from seeing Natalie, and there is no outbreak. Nothing will be reported downtown, and our jobs are safe. He started dancing around. Samantha had never seen him this happy. However, she was in no mood for him today. She just watched him make a fool of himself, all the time wishing he would just get the heck out of her office.

After finishing his performance, he gave a deep bow, took his leave and headed back to his office. He felt like clicking his heels together—he felt that good.

As his office came in sight, he realized the outer door was partially opened, and Laura his secretary was nowhere in sight. He called out her name, but got no response. He looked around for signs of an intruder and seeing no one, he entered. He again called out for Laura, but just like before he received no reply.

"I wonder where she could be, and why did she leave the door unlocked? I need to have a long talk with her about keeping the office door closed. This is unacceptable. There are so many important documents here. Anyone could just walk in and take them," he said.

Still feeling a bit shaken, he passed through to his office still listening and looking around for signs of an intruder. He could see no one lurking about, but the first thing that caught his eyes was a manila envelope lying on his desk. This in itself was not unusual, because on any given day, as the hospital administrator, he could be bombarded with over a dozen pieces of mail. Laura would routinely review his mail and address those that did not require his attention. She would only place those requiring his personal attention on his desk.

Another reason why this envelope stood out was that, as a rule, envelopes used for inter-hospital mail were multi-used and each recipient's name was handwritten. This envelope was brand new and his name was typewritten.

He carefully picked up the envelope by one corner and examined it. There was no return address and no postage, which could only mean that it had been hand delivered. He shook it to see if it emitted any sounds. He tried to see if any unusual odor emanated from it, but nothing gave him any clue as to where it had originated.

He felt the contents through the envelope, trying to guess what was inside. He could see the outline of a rectangular object, almost the size of an audio-tape. After much procrastination, he decided that there was only one way to find out what it contained.

"What's the worst that could happen?" he asked himself. "It's not as if I have enemies who would send me a letter bomb." He gave a nervous laugh.

Locating his letter opener, he angrily ripped open the envelope.

His guess was right. A small audiotape wrapped in a single sheet of white typing paper fell onto his desk.

His knees started shaking so he decided he should sit before he fell.

He reached for the paper. It was a letter addressed to him in bold type.

He started reading.

Brandon,

You don't remember me, but I remember you quite well. Just imagine! You're now the big man on campus. Who would have thought?

I have been observing you for a while now, and I must say you have turned out to be quite an interesting man. I would like you to meet me at five o'clock today at that little Italian restaurant not far from the hospital. You know the one—Maroni's.

If you're interested in keeping that fancy job of yours, make sure you keep our date, and don't keep me waiting. You won't like the outcome if you do. Don't worry. I'll recognize you. Just sit at your usual table and I'll find you.

One last thing: Make sure you take your medicine before you meet me, and re-member to always keep your office door closed.

See you real soon,

An old friend

P.S. I have extra copies of the tape, so even if you destroy this one, I have others. See you later, old friend.

Brandon's mind was a jumble of thoughts as he finished reading. The letter fell from his hands, but he was unaware. He snatched open his desk drawer and searched around until he found an old tape recorder stashed way in the back.

"I knew this would come in handy one day," he mumbled.

His hand trembled as he fumbled to insert the tape. As it snapped into place, he hit the rewind button. There was no need. It was queued to play. He did not have long to wait.

He sat, mesmerized at the sound of his own voice:

I'm stagnating. I'm fifty-five years old, and I've worked my tail off for this or-ganization for the past five years. What more can I do to prove my allegiance to this organization? I'm Brandon Saunders, and it's time for me to move on up to the big leagues. I want to play with the big boys and call the shots. Soon I'll be chair of the most powerful health care organization in the city, and nothing or no one is going to stop me. It's time I put my plans in motion.

I did all of this. When I got here, there was nothing more than a small dilapi-dated, one-story building. I have fought for this, and I expect to get paid.

I have to be more careful. I can't let them know my plans, or someone will steal them.

Brandon had heard enough. He slowly reached over and pushed the off button, placed his head in his hands, and cried like a baby.

Solange Matthews

Solange had been in the department long enough, and to everyone's delight, had adapted amazingly well. Because of her quiet demeanor, Natalie had been unsure if Solange would fit in with the demands of the busy department. However, Solange had surprised everyone and was now proving to be one of the most dependable ICN's in the department.

She was now more relaxed and talkative and quite capable of defending herself, especially when her nemesis Velma went on the attack.

As her orientation progressed, Solange was gradually given more and more responsibilities, which she embraced wholeheartedly. Because she had a solid background in medicine, Natalie had assigned her to the rehabilitation service which fell under the umbrella of the medical services.

In addition to their own units, ICN's were responsible for each other's department during vacation time, sick days, while attending conferences, or any other reasons for absences. Therefore an overall knowledge of all areas was a requirement and extremely beneficial, especially if one had plans to become certified in the area of infection control. To help acquire knowledge about these services, policy manuals were always available for reference. To gain some surgical experience, Solange was assigned to the orthopedic service, which consisted of inpatient as well as outpatient clinics.

The rehab unit was located in the newest part of the building and was usually very quiet in terms of resistant organisms. However, one or more patients requiring isolation could generally be found on the unit. These patients were either transferred from other units to receive rehab or they were sometimes admitted with a history of prior resistant organisms.

The usual culprits were organisms such as MRSA, which was usually acquired in the community. On rare occasions, there might be a case of shingles or even a case of penicillin-resistant *Streptococcus pneumoniae*. Regardless of the name of the organism, as long as it was classified as being resistant, Infection Control was generally notified, and a visit could be expected from an ICN.

The type of isolation required was always dependent on the organism and the route of spread. However, the bar could never be lowered, and vigilance always had to be maintained in order to prevent and control infectious spread.

• • •

One organism that has caused major concern recently is MRSA.

Although most MRSA infections do not tend to be serious, some can be life threatening. Because this bug is now more prevalently seen in the community, policy makers have recommended that all patients admitted to healthcare facilities be screened for MRSA on admission and on discharge. Not only is this bug present in healthcare facilities, but it is now seen in prisons, schools, and nursing homes, or wherever large groups congregate. Patients with open wounds, invasive devices, and weakened immune systems are at greater risk of infection than persons with intact immune systems.

The symptoms of MRSA will often depend on the location of the infection. Most often, it causes only a mild skin infection such as sores or boils. However, it can become more serious, infecting surgical wounds, the lungs, the bloodstream, or even the urinary tract.

Because of the difficulty in treating this organism, MRSA is sometimes called a "super bug," and many public health experts have become alarmed by the rapid spread of tough strains of this organism. Because of the overabundant use of antibiotics, it will take both knowledge and a serving of vigilance on the part of everyone—healthcare workers and the general public—in order to curb this menace.

• • •

The best survival strategy for any ICN depends on which trick she has up her sleeve on any given day. One of the best strategy is the timing of unit rounds. Solange had received this piece of advice very early during her orientation period. The element of surprise never grows old. *Never make unit rounds at the same time each day.* It was always the hope that an unscheduled appearance would keep staff on their toes and prevent them from breaking the rules.

Solange reviewed the new admissions from the previous day, then made her way to the rehab unit to visit two new patients. This was the second admission for the first patient who was a 40-year-old male named Clarence

Simon. He had previously sustained a fractured left leg during an accident and had been hospitalized for ten days. During his previous stay, he had been diagnosed with MRSA in the injured leg and had received appropriate antibiotics prior to discharge. His wound was clean and partially closed on discharge, however, he needed to be re-admitted.

The second patient was a homeless, 55-year-old male named David Smith. Not only was he physically unkempt, but the odor of an infected wound was quite evident to trained nostrils. His admitting physical exam showed an open, draining abdominal wound, which he claimed he had sustained during an altercation with a knife-wielding friend. Based on their admission history of draining wounds, fever, and elevated white blood count, Solange wanted to see for herself how they were being housed. In addition, cultures had been obtained on admission, and even though the final results were not yet available and no specific organisms identified, she wanted to take a proactive approach.

As she entered the unit, she observed that one of the new patients was housed in a single room, while the other was sharing a room with another patient.

Justice was in the process of converting all paper charts to electronic records. However this was a time consuming process, and some sections were incomplete. These included the physicians' notes and other consults; therefore a physical chart was still available for review of certain portions of the patient care record.

After greeting the staff, Solange located the chart for both patients, and then logged on to an unoccupied computer. As soon as she located Mr. Simon's chart, an Alert screen popped up, identifying the patient as having had MRSA. Before proceeding any further, she located the head nurse.

"Gabriel, who's caring for Mr. Simon today?" Solange asked.

"He's the new admission, right?" asked Gabriel, consulting her assignment form. "Nurse Collins. Why?"

Solange ignored the question. "What time was he admitted?"

"Nine o'clock last night."

"Has Nurse Collins done her chart review?" Solange asked.

"Yes, she has to do that before starting her patient care," Gabriel replied, looking questioningly at Solange.

Still wondering why Solange was asking these questions, Gabriel asked nervously, "Why? Did she do something wrong?"

Looking at the opened computer screen, Solange pointed to the Alert screen that had popped up when she accessed the patient's record. "Do you see this? Do you know what it means?" she asked.

"Yes, I know what it means," Gabriel said.

Solange waited expectantly for Gabriel to explain what the Alert meant.

As Gabriel hesitated, Solange asked, "So, what does it mean?"

Gabriel moved closer to the computer and commenced reading silently. When she finished reading, she realized that she was not as familiar with the Alert as she had thought. She felt a bit foolish and said as much.

"Solange, I'm sorry, but I didn't realize what that sign meant," Gabriel said. "I guess we sometimes overlook some things in order to complete the admission and move on quickly to other things."

Solage knew an impromptu in-service was called for, and there was no time like the present.

"That's quite okay. I'm glad that you acknowledged that you don't know. Now that I know, I can do something about it. Can you get the staff together? I'd like to review this with everyone," Solange said.

The staff quickly gathered around the nursing station anxiously awaiting Solange's in-service.

"Okay. We're a large medical center, and as such, there are always going to be patients readmitted. It's just part of the business that we do. When a patient with a history of a resistant organism is readmitted, an Alert screen will pop up as soon as the demographical data is entered. This screen was installed by the Informational Technology Department at the request of the Infection Control Department. It serves to alert nursing staff when a patient had a resistant organism in the past.

"This information is usually entered by an ICN at the time the patient is first diagnosed, and it remains there until the patient is no longer infected. This information is or should be accessed at the time the patient is admitted to the ER. In case it's missed by the ER staff, then the staff on the admitting unit should recognize this and take the necessary action."

"What steps should we take Solange?" one staff member asked.

"That's a very good question. If the patient has a draining wound or a fever, then that patient should be placed in a single room and a 'contact isolation' sign placed on the door to his room. A culture of the wound must be obtained. If the result is positive, then you're already one-step ahead and would've prevented any transmission to others.

"However if the results are negative, then you need to determine where his placement should be. He can remain in a single room, however, if there are other patients who have a more urgent need for that single room, then he can be placed in a multi-bedded room. He can't, however, be placed in a room with a fresh post-op patient. Remember to adhere to all aspects of standard precautions," Solange explained.

As Solange looked around at the faces before her, they clearly reflected they had learned something new that day. "Are there any questions?' she asked.

No one answered.

"Don't forget, I'm always available to answer your questions. You can reach me by phone, or you can have me paged. There's never a stupid question, and I'd prefer that you call and ask rather than run the risk of exposing a patient or yourselves to a resistant organism. Thanks, everybody," Solange said.

As she headed back to the office, she felt, at last, she was doing what she loved. She was an educator, not just for the patients, but also to the staff.

Brandon Saunders 33

After a good long bout of crying, Brandon got up from his desk.

"This is not helping," he said angrily. "I will not give in to some unknown blackmailer. I will not grant him the courtesy of meeting with him."

A quick glance at his watch told him it was either time to go home, or time to meet with his blackmailer. Shrugging into his coat, he realized that he was shaking all over. Fear was about to overcome his resolution, and he could not afford to show fear, so he removed his coat and sat back down.

"Blackmailers can smell fear a mile away. I need to think this through. I can't afford to be too hasty," he told himself.

At 5:00 in the evening, Maroni's was jumping. Great tasting food has a way of selling itself and one could not find better tasting Italian food than at Maroni's. No wonder it was so well supported by the employees of Justice.

The bar area was crowded and noisy. The after work hospital crowd was pouring in, trying to forget their hectic day by drowning it out with alcohol. Alcohol also worked wonders for the cold weather, so it was a win-win all around, whichever way you looked at it.

A dark complexioned man with dark, piercing eyes sat at a table in the back. His age was indeterminate, and he looked as if life had not been too good to him. He was tall and thin, and he looked as if he could do with a good meal and a hot bath. On the table, he carefully nursed a can of Budweiser, as if he wanted it to last for a very long time.

He did not mingle with the other revelers, but was very much aware of the ongoing chaos, and even smiled on occasion at some off-color humor.

From time to time, he glanced at the door as if expecting company. When he was not glancing at the door, he was looking at the wall clock.

At exactly six o'clock, he gave one last look at the clock, angrily snatched up his coat and backpack and elbowed his way out the door. Reaching the sidewalk, he dialed a number on his cell phone and waited impatiently.

"You'd better answer if you know what's good for you," he said, tapping his foot angrily.

The call went straight to voicemail:

You've reached the office of Brandon Saunders. Sorry I missed your call. Your call is very important to me, so please leave a message at the sound of the beep, and I'll return your call as soon as possible. Have a wonderful day!

He was so angry, he couldn't wait for the beep to end. "So you think you're so smart, eh? You think you can ignore me? How dare you stand me up? I'm a nice guy, so I'll give you another chance. You'll be hearing from me," he said.

He flipped his phone closed and hurriedly walked north toward the bus stop.

Brandon Saunders 34

Brandon spent a sleepless night, tossing and turning, unable to turn his brain off. His mind ran scenarios of who might be his blackmailer.

"Of course I may have stepped on a few toes in my climb to this position, but doesn't everyone? It's all part of the dirty game of politics! No big deal!" he said to himself.

But who would be so vindictive as to want to see him destroyed?

After tossing and turning for what seemed like hours, he got up and headed toward his home office. It was large and spacious and the most comfortable space in his condo. He had spent a bundle having it designed to his specifications, and he did his best thinking in this sanctuary space.

Not many people knew this about him, but he was an avid lover of classical music, a taste he had developed over the years. He enjoyed the soothing sounds from Bach to Beethoven, but he was also not averse to listening to some wave sounds on a Caribbean beach.

Tonight he was in the mood for Bach. As he relaxed on his chaise surrounded by the relaxing sounds of Bach's *Air on a G String*, he was transported to a whole other space. Soon his mind was free and clear, and his problems started drifting away.

The sound of the telephone broke through his reverie.

He decided to let it ring. After all it was now 2:30 in the morning.

"Who could be calling at this time of night?" he asked himself. "I need my beauty sleep." He turned impatiently, this time lying on his side away from the phone. Returning to his music, he tried to focus, but the mood was already lost. The phone finally stopped ringing, but no message was left.

He looked at the phone screen, but did not recognize the caller's number.

"Maybe it's a wrong number, or someone who couldn't sleep either." He yawned as he headed back to the bedroom to try and get some sleep before heading in to work.

At six o'clock, the alarm went off. Being a creature of habit, he threw back the covers and dragged himself out of bed. He felt like he'd been run over by a ten-ton truck.

"Strong, hot coffee is just what I need," he told himself as he headed toward the kitchen. Soon he was on his second cup and still felt as if a thick fog surrounded his brain.

"There's no way I can function at work today. I need to take the day off," he said.

Sitting at his kitchen island, he was suddenly hit with the magnitude of what he was facing. Someone was trying to take his job away, someone who claimed he knew him. He needed some help dealing with this. He could not handle this on his own.

He had the number for his therapist on speed dial, so he hit the number and anxiously waited for the person at the other end to pick up.

The ringing of the phone awakened Celeste from a beautiful dream. She glanced at her bedside clock, annoyed that it was a just a few minutes after 6:00. She debated whether she should answer it or not, having only gone to bed at two o'clock. She thought to herself, *Maybe one of my patients is in trouble.* With this thought running through her head, she reached for the phone.

"Celeste Portman. How can I help you?" said a soft-spoken voice with a British accent.

Not realizing he was holding his breath, Brandon breathed out deeply.

"Hello Celeste, this is Brandon Saunders. I know my appointment is not until next week, but I really need to talk with you today. What time can I come in?"

"Brandon, I have a very tight schedule today, I need to look at my appointment book before I can answer that," Celeste said.

"Okay, I'll hold," Brandon replied.

"No, I'll get back to you in…say an hour. Is that alright with you?"

Thinking he had no other choice, he said, "Okay, I'll be waiting."

He pushed the off button and waited.

Natalie Sinclair

As Natalie anxiously awaited the results of her neurological tests, her mind created a million different scenarios. Over the last few days, her headaches had lessened, and for a while, she even forgot that she had been having problems. She was so focused on the preparation for the upcoming JCAHO survey, she had chosen to ignore any and all minor discomfort.

Steve however, was the exact opposite. From the moment he realized that Natalie was experiencing health problems, not a day went by that he did not worry. He worried to the point that he refused for Natalie to drive to and from work, so he had arranged for a car service to take her back and forth.

Of course, this annoyed Natalie to no end, seeing this as nothing less than an infringement on her independence and a major inconvenience. Nevertheless, Steve held his ground and refused to budge.

"Until I hear from David that everything is fine, I do not want you driving on the highway. If you try to, I promise I'll take away your car keys," Steve had told her angrily, and from his tone, Natalie knew that he meant every word.

"When will David have the results? It's been a week now," Natalie asked becoming more and more frustrated.

They were in the kitchen rushing through breakfast before heading off to work.

"I understand your frustration. I will talk to David today and see what the hold-up is." Grabbing his coat, Steve gave her a hurried kiss. "I have to go. I'll call you later," he said as he headed out the door.

Her car service was already waiting in the driveway, so Natalie hurried out and was soon on her way to Justice.

So much has already been done, but there is still so much more to do in preparing for JCAHO, she thought to herself.

She entered her office to the sound of her phone ringing. She hurriedly picked up the receiver before it went to voicemail. Before she said "hello," she recognized Steve's voice speaking to someone at his end. Realizing that Natalie had picked up at her end, Steve quickly greeted her.

"Hi, Nat. I was just talking to David…" He did not finish the sentence before Natalie jumped in.

"What did he say? What are the results of the MRI?" she asked, trying hard to keep her voice from quivering.

"The MRI was non-specific, so he wants to repeat it. This time he would like to do an MRI with contrast," Steve said.

"Why?" Natalie asked.

"Well, performing an MRI using a contrast media will help to improve the visibility of structures in the brain. It will provide a clearer image of the parts of the brain that can't be seen with a plain MRI."

Natalie did not respond. Steve became worried.

"Natalie, are you there?" he asked.

She breathed deeply before speaking. "I'm here, Steve. I just need to process all of this. I think I'll have to wait until after JCAHO before I'll have time to get this done. There is just too much to do deal with right now," Natalie said.

Steve could hear the tears in her voice and was doing his best not to fall apart himself.

"What exactly did David see or not see that he feels there's a need to repeat the MRI using contrast?" she asked, clearing her throat.

"Well, he did not see anything specific. That's why he wants to be sure before we get our hopes raised or dashed to pieces," Steve said.

He wanted so badly to lighten the mood and move on to a different subject, but he could not find a way, so he quickly asked, "Anyway, how are you feeling? How's your head?"

She desperately wanted to tell him that she had felt better before his call, but she fought hard to hold it back. So she calmly replied, "I'm good. My head feels fine right now. Let's hope it stays that way the rest of the day."

"I'm happy to hear that. I'll talk to you later," Steve said.

Natalie reached into her pocket book for her pain pills, popped two into her mouth, followed by a large glass of water.

Brandon Saunders 36

Celeste finally called Brandon to let him know there was a cancellation, so she would see him in her office at ten o'clock. He couldn't wait. Four hours of waiting seemed like a lifetime. He turned the shower to the hottest temperature he could tolerate and closed his eyes, hoping to erase the tension that had taken possession of his neck and shoulders. He followed that with a large cup of strong, black coffee.

He breathed deeply as the hot liquid found its way into his stomach, and the caffeine began to work its magic.

"That really hits the spot," he said as he moved his head back and forth.

Soon it was time to head to Celeste's office. He was never more grateful to see her in his life. He had been seeing her for the greater part of two years now, and each time he left her office, his euphoria was unbounded. When he had first decided to see a therapist, he had done some intense research to find just the right person he would connect with, and so far, he had never regretted his decision to stick with Celeste.

Some of his top requirements when he was looking for a therapist included the therapist's ability to be friendly and to make him feel comfortable. He had actually visited the offices of several other therapists before he made the decision to see Celeste on a regular basis.

What also helped in his decision to have her as his therapist was the condition of her office. To some the reason might seem trite, but he knew what he wanted, and he felt it was important in the pursuit of his peace of mind. Not only was her office clean and orderly, but it contained some personal touches, such as throw pillows, diplomas hanging on the wall, and some family photos. This gave the office a nice, warm, comfortable, and inviting feel.

In addition, it had a homey and softer feel because of the presence of the tastefully placed cushioned chairs, carpeting, table lamps, plants, and throw rugs. Although cost had never been an obstacle, he realized her fees were less than some of the others he had visited and was in fact quite affordable, not to mention that Celeste was quite a looker and very easy on the eyes. He would never ever think of hitting on his therapist—that was a definite no—but it certainly did not hurt to have some beautiful eye candy. Plus he was a sucker for that British accent.

Brandon made himself comfortable while Celeste settled in and consulted her notes before making eye contact.

"So Brandon, you sounded quite upset when you called. What's going on?" she started off. Brandon squirmed inside, realizing he had never voiced his present problems to anyone since it had all started.

"Where do I start?' he asked staring at the opposite wall.

"The beginning is always a good place," she said smiling.

"Good idea," he replied nervously. "Yesterday I received an anonymous letter…" He began.

He stumbled through his story and finished off by telling her that he had not shown up for the appointment with the blackmailer.

"Have you notified the police?" asked Celeste.

"No, I thought I would talk to you first," he said.

"I think it's a matter for the police. You need to think this through very carefully. Do you have enough medication on hand, or do I need to call Dr. Simon for a refill?"

"I have enough. Thanks," Brandon said.

Celeste gave him her full attention while he unburdened himself, intervening only when necessary. By the end of the session, Brandon felt lighter, and he had made his decision about how to handle the blackmailer. He left the office in a much better frame of mind, ready to deal with the upcoming JCAHO survey.

As soon as Brandon left the office, Celeste reviewed her notes. From past experience, she knew Brandon was very clever at telling her what he thought she wanted to hear, but she was onto him, and he did not fool her for a minute. Based on what he had revealed to her, she was deeply worried for him and his safety. There was nothing she could do however. The laws concerning patient confidentiality were very rigid, and she had no intention of breaking them. She did, however, plan to stay in close contact with Brandon over the next few weeks to make sure he was safe and would not do anything foolish to jeopardize his health or wellbeing.

JCAHO Survey 37

March was finally here and the dreaded JCAHO survey was scheduled to begin on Monday of the third week. It was scheduled to last four days, and everyone hoped that it would go smoothly. This survey encompassed the entire medical center, so the levels of adrenaline ran high throughout the entire facility.

Weeks before the actual date, the entire campus was a constant buzz of activity, and departments that had not seen a coat of paint in a long time were now so sparkling clean, you could eat off the floor. It was important that the hospital receive this much sought after three-year accreditation in order to remain in good standing and be competitive with other institutions.

As the transformation of the buildings and grounds took place, you could hear the question being asked over and over again: "Why is it so difficult to keep it looking this nice all the time? This would avoid so much craziness at survey time." Of course there was never an answer, and three years later when another survey was due, you would again hear the same question being asked.

The JCAHO is a private, nonprofit organization whose mission is to continuously improve the safety and quality of healthcare provided to the public.

Receiving JCAHO accreditation shows that hospitals and other healthcare providers have mastered the process of providing the highest level of service to their consumers; it's like a feather in one's cap.

However, preparing for a JCAHO survey can be a tedious and challenging process. The JCAHO standards are published annually and are available on the organization's website for download by any facility desiring to have the survey process. The facility being surveyed must be able to examine its current processes, policies, and all procedures relevant to the JCAHO standards. They must also be prepared to improve any areas that are not currently in compliance with the standards.

Employees must also be familiar with the standards and practices relevant to the department in which they work, and they must be prepared to address them if and when questioned by a surveyor.

Even though there are other organizations that can grant accreditation to a healthcare facility, the JCAHO is by far the largest and most prestigious, so most organizations strive toward receiving it.

To obtain accreditation, staff members in healthcare organizations must be able to demonstrate proficiency based on specific job competencies. In addition, they must also receive performance evaluations based on their specific job descriptions.

Obtaining JCAHO accreditation definitely provides a competitive edge in the marketplace. Adhering to the standards allows the facility to strive for quality improvement in safety and overall healthcare for patients and families. It is also recognized by most insurers and third parties, and it is a mandatory requirement in some states.

• • •

It had been about two months since the infection control team had been meeting to review the JCAHO infection control standards, but the meetings had increased to weekly as the time drew closer. The staff had been drilled in every aspect of their daily tasks, and Natalie had offered them encouragement every step of the way.

At each meeting, she would remind them, "Don't be nervous. Just think of what you do on a daily basis and respond accordingly. You know this. You've been doing this for years."

Of course this was easier said than done. Everyone felt confident as far as performing their tasks were concerned; the nervousness and anxiety lay in the thought that they might actually be called upon to speak on the day of the departmental conference.

JCAHO Survey 38

Monday morning finally arrived, and word started spreading like wild fire throughout the facility that the surveyors were actually on the premises. As was the rule, the surveyors' first meeting was with the leadership, who included the hospital administrators, directors of Environment of Care, Information Management, Human Resources, Performance Improvement, Emergency Management, Life Safety, and other department directors.

During this meeting, the surveyors first verified that the survey had begun and then downloaded the survey agenda. They were then escorted to the conference room, which was set aside for them to work undisturbed. They were provided with all the amenities needed to make them comfortable: the best brands of coffee, tea, juices, bottled water, and unlimited and various types of snacks.

After requesting the documents that would be used during the survey, they began with an opening conference and an orientation to the facility. This meeting lasted approximately one hour and consisted of an interactive discussion in which the surveyors described the structure of the survey and answered any questions about the survey activities.

The surveyors then tried to gain knowledge about how the organization is structured and how it operates. This information will ultimately help to ensure a relevant and credible survey for the facility, and it will be used by the surveyors to select individual patients for follow-up later, a process referred to as "tracer activity."

As news that the surveyors are on site quickly traveled throughout the medical center, adrenaline levels increased by tenfold!

The surveyors spent the next hour and a half doing "individual tracing" with one or more patients. They tried to determine the patient's experience with the organization to evaluate the organization's compliance with standards as they related to the care and services provided. In addition, they reviewed the patient's record and visited with the patient and interviewed assigned staff members.

Different teams had spent months viewing and reviewing assigned patients' records to ensure that everything was ready for this day. Survey time was no time to discover that relevant and important documents had been omitted or misfiled.

Everyone prayed that today would not be the day!

Lunchtime soon arrived and a gourmet meal was provided in the executive dining room. Appealing to the gastronomical side of guests who hold the future of your institutions in the palms of their hands does no one any harm!

"Oohs" and "ahs" were not in short supply at the sight of the tastefully decorated bounty set before the surveyors, however only half an hour could be spared to enjoy this culinary delight.

Soon they were again involved in a process known as "system tracers," which is an interactive discussion between assigned staff and the surveyors. It is intended to help the surveyors evaluate the organization's compliance to standards as they relate to the systems and processes used to support patient care activities.

Depending on the services provided, invited staff might include, but was not limited to, representatives from: Data Management, Infection Control, Environment of Care, Medication Management, Equipment Management, Hospital Readmission, Billing, and Regulatory Review.

Next in line was a one-hour leadership session. This consisted of an interactive discussion between the leadership of the organization and the surveyors. It was designed to explore the leadership's responsibility for creating and maintaining the structure and the key processes that contribute to the quality and safety of the care, treatment, or services provided.

The end of day one arrived, and there were three more to go!

The surveyors made their departure, leaving management and staff to spend yet another sleepless night. Tomorrow would be the start of the visits to the different areas selected by the surveyors. These visits would determine whether or not the structures and key processes previously discussed were indeed being implemented!

JCAHO Survey

During any JCAHO survey, knowledge of some unwritten rules will prove beneficial to staff in the long run. Breaking any of these rules is strongly frowned upon and almost tantamount to treason. Here are the rules:

1. Calling in sick during survey week is not an option. Unless you are on your deathbed, and your doctor calls to report that you only have a few hours to live, then you had better be at work.
2. Requesting vacation during survey week is frowned upon.
3. If you have a relative in a distant country who is on the verge of dying, inform your relatives to try and find a way to keep that person alive. If your loved one has just died, it would be best if you ask your living relatives to hold off on the funeral until the end of survey.
4. If in the past you were consistently late for work, find a way to be on time during survey week.

However, there are exceptions to every rule:

If you are borderline functional, someone who always says or does the wrong thing at the wrong time, resulting in chaos and embarrassment for your unit and the hospital, you are encouraged to take your vacation during survey week. No one wants to look incompetent, flustered, or ill-informed in front of a JCAHO surveyor. You will never be able to live it down!

For the staff member who breaks out in a cold sweat at the mere sight of a surveyor, they have found very innovative ways of keeping out of sight.

It is not unheard of to keep busy behind a bedside curtain while surveyors are on a unit. After all, privacy is a patient's right, not a privilege. Surveyors are professionals, and it is not their intent to deprive a patient of care. Therefore they would not interrupt during the rendering of care to an incontinent patient, in order to ask a question of a staff member.

Stress and anxiety affects everyone in different ways and plays a major role in how the body responds. The sudden onset of diarrhea, resulting in spending a lot of time in the staff bathroom, is not an uncommon occurrence. Nose bleeds and asthma attacks are rare, but have had their fair share of playing major roles in JCAHO tragedies. Overall, no one has ever met their demise as a result of a survey.

There are other creative methods that have been used to avoid having a one to one with a surveyor, but all in all it is always better to be up to date with one's organizational policies, rather than having to expend one's energy on avoidance tactics.

JCAHO Survey

Tuesday and Wednesday slowly dragged by, and the rumors kept flying:

"Did you hear that the Dietary Department got cited for thawing poultry under hot running water?

"I heard that the Linen Department got cited for sorting dirty laundry on the floor.

"Did you hear that a nurse was observed not washing her hands after she removed her soiled gloves?

"I heard that one employee was not wearing the correct mask while caring for a patient in isolation!"

On and on it went! No one really sure which rumor was true and which was not.

Regardless of the rumors, the surveyed department would breathe a sigh of relief, knowing they had made it through the fire and survived. At least for now!

• • •

One can always hope and pray, but it is not within our power to postpone a day from arriving any more than we can cause it to rain. So inevitably, Thursday morning arrived!

This was the last day of the survey, and the day that the infection control team would meet with the surveyors.

One by one the ICPs begin to arrive. As they made their way into the office, the sun was playing peek-a-boo, hiding in and out behind the clouds. The wind was brisk, sending a chill all the way to the very bones.

But it was the month of March, so what else could be expected?

Every eye was tearing, every nose running, and every cheek reddened as they wended their way to the office from the parking lot.

"Miracles are still happening. You can see my red cheeks through my black skin," said Rochelle laughingly, while wiping her runny nose.

Trying to warm their hands, Kirsten and Lisa gathered around the old radiator, which had been turned off overnight. It was old and took a while before the water started flowing to bring some warmth to the coils.

"I can't even remove my gloves, my fingers are so frozen," said Lisa, her teeth chattering loudly.

"I know," replied Kirsten, shivering though her many layers of clothing. "I had to put on some long johns this morning. Do you know the last time I wore long johns? I had to search hard to find them. In addition, I have on my underwear, T-shirt, sweater, jacket and coat, two pairs of socks, plus my boots. I feel like Frosty the Snowwoman. If I fall down, there is no way I would be able to get up on my own," she started laughing. "They'll just have to roll me the rest of the way," she continued.

Tears were streaming down their cheeks as they all joined in laughing.

"I'll go you one better," said Lisa, barely able to catch her breath, she was laughing so hard. "In addition to all you just mentioned, I have on two pair of gloves, ear muffs, a hat with ear flaps, and two scarves, and I'm still cold!"

By then the entire staff, hearing the laughter, had joined in. So Natalie was surprised when she walked into the small kitchen and saw her staff trying hard not to have an accident from laughing so hard.

She smiled, happy to see everyone in such a good mood. "I guess you guys are all ready for your interviews," she said.

That was enough to break the mood and bring everyone back to the reality of what lay ahead. The laughter abruptly ceased. By then they were all feeling a bit warmer as the radiator had started making snapping, crackling, and popping sounds, just like the cereal.

The interview for the department was scheduled from 1:00 to 1:30. Until then, only the basic and most essential work would be done, as no one would be able to concentrate on anything but the upcoming interview.

"Would anyone like to review, or do you feel ready?" Natalie asked, emerging from her office.

In unison, everyone called out, "No more review. We feel overwhelmed."

"My head is bursting. If I do anymore review, I'm going to mess everything up," Lisa replied.

Rochelle joined in, "No more please. I just want to get this over and done with."

Not to be outdone, Kirsten joined in, "More review will just confuse me more and make me realize how much I don't know."

Natalie raised her hands in submission and started walking away.

"Okay, okay, no more review. Candace, please make sure you bring the policy manual and the survey binder when you go down. Remember, everyone, please be on time."

"Where are we meeting again, Natalie?" asked Lisa

"The conference room on the first floor. Room three west to be specific. It's large enough to accommodate everyone. You guys should only make rounds today if there's an emergency. Have an early lunch, and again, don't be late." Natalie's last words were said smilingly, but her eyes were focused directly on Rochelle.

Her meaning was not lost on anyone.

Infection Control Interview

It was now half past twelve and the tension was palpable in the office as the staff prepared for their interview. One by one, they headed for the ladies room, some to make a last minute deposit of number one or two, but all wanting to freshen up and look their best. On the outside, they all wanted to appear calm and assured, but everyone who knew them, especially Natalie, knew that on the inside they were all quivering like bowls of jelly.

"Kirsten, you don't need all that makeup. Where do you think you're going?" asked Rochelle laughingly.

"Do you really think it's too much?" Kirsten asked nervously, looking at herself in the mirror. "I guess I'll take some off."

She hurriedly pulled a hand towel from the dispenser, moistened it under running water, and began rubbing vigorously at her lips. She realized she needed to use the restroom before heading out to the conference room, so she decided she could do both at the same time; multi-tasking as it were. She finished on the toilet and headed back to the sink. Before she looked at herself in the mirror, she asked Rochelle, "Is this better?"

Rochelle turned, took one look at Kirsten's face and burst out laughing.

"Why are you laughing?" Kirsten asked angrily.

"Look in the mirror," said Rochelle pointing and continuing to laugh.

Kirsten took one look at her lips, and to her dismay, the blood red lipstick had migrated to a significant portion of both her upper and lower lips. Unfortunately, the continued scrubbing had also caused some irritation around her lips, which was quite visible to any observer.

"Oh my word. What am I going to do?" she cried almost tearfully.

"Don't worry Kirsten, you can fix it, I'm sure."

She quickly dug into her makeup bag, not sure of what she was looking for, but hoping against hope that a miracle would happen. She pulled out some lip balm and applied it to the blood red lipstick that had spread to her upper and lower lips. The lip balm did nothing to correct the problem.

By now the other nurses had come in to see what Rochelle was laughing about. As they crowded into the small restroom, they just had to take one look at Kirsten. They couldn't help themselves either and soon the restroom reverberated with the sound of laughter.

On her way to the conference room, Natalie overheard the noise. She had been wondering where the nurses had disappeared to, knowing they would not want to enter the conference room without her. As she entered the bathroom, one look told her all she needed to know. It was a sight to behold. Try as she could, she could not withhold a smile.

"Ladies, it's time to go. Kirsten, I'm not sure what to tell you, but please try your best and fix your face. We can't all be late, so the rest of you please get your things together and let's go."

She held the door open while the rest of the staff headed for the office to gather their documents to meet with the surveyors.

Feeling sorry for Kirsten, Rochelle whispered to her before exiting. "Here Kirsten, maybe you can find something in here that can help." She handed her makeup kit to Kirsten with a gentle, "Good luck."

Kirsten accepted it gratefully, not sure what she could do with African American makeup. The colors were so much darker than what she normally used. However, out of sheer desperation, she decided to take a look inside Rochelle's bag. She opened the bag and removed the bottle of liquid makeup.

"This is so dark, I'm really not sure," she said to herself.

Then as if a light bulb went off in her head, she brightened up. Taking the dark make up, she applied a light coat over the skin around her lips, followed by a light coat of her regular shade. She worked them both into her skin and the more she applied the combination, the more pleased she became with the result. She continued until her entire face reflected that of someone just returning from a Caribbean vacation. She applied a pastel shade lipstick and then hurried out to join her teammates in the conference room.

It was 12:55 and everyone was gathered around the large conference room table anxiously awaiting the arrival of the nurse who would conduct the interview. There was light chatter all around, mostly to ward off the anxiety that the occasion usually provoked.

Each time the door opened, the chatter would cease, only to quickly resume when they saw who entered. However, when Kirsten entered, not only did the chatter cease, but before it resumed, the surveyor entered the room. All eyes were focused on Kirsten, all wondering if they were looking at a new staff member. However, no one had a chance to talk with her, as Ms. Carlyle the administrator escorted the surveyor into the room. She made sure she was comfortably seated before occupying the chair next to her. She cleared her throat.

Everyone came to attention.

"Hello everyone. Thank you all for coming. Let me introduce Ms. McNally," Ms. Carlyle acknowledged the surveyor and then continued.

"Ms. McNally will be conducting the infection control interview. Let's start by having each person introduce themselves, and please state the department which you are representing."

Ms. Carlyle looked to her right, indicating a point from which to start.

"Samantha Brown, Chief Nurse Executive."

"Brandon Saunders, Hospital Administrator."

"Natalie Sinclair, Director of Infection Control."

"Elizabeth Corbin, Chair of Infection Control Committee."

"Frances Molloy, Director of Bacteriology."

By the end of the introductions, all the key departments were represented. Among those were the directors of Environmental Services, Pharmacy, Medical and Surgical ICU, Nursing Education, and many others, making a total of twenty individuals.

There was a hush at the end of the introductions. Everyone seemed to be busy trying to read the surveyor's thoughts, wondering who would be the first lamb called to the slaughter.

After having attended many survey conferences, many sitting around the table were well aware not to judge a book by its cover. The surveyor had a pleasant demeanor, and everyone hoped this would be conveyed during the session and especially during the final summation. Of course nothing could be taken for granted, and therefore no one could afford to sit on their laurels until the final day of summation.

Looking at Natalie, Ms. McNally asked, "How many ICPs are there in your department?"

"There are six plus myself," Natalie replied.

"And how many beds are there?"

"We have a total of eight hundred beds."

"What's your occupancy rate," Ms. McNally asked, turning to Brandon Saunders.

"About 95 percent," he replied.

Returning to Natalie, she continued. "You seem to be very well staffed. Are you involved in a lot of projects?"

"Yes we are. As you know, the most recent recommendations from the CDC's National Nosocomial Infections Surveillance System (NNIS) require one full-time infection control professional for the first one hundred beds and then one for each additional two hundred fifty beds. In addition, our community has a large population of homeless and elderly residents, so we have our share of community-acquired infections in addition to other surveillance activities. We can show you our surveillance activities for the past…"

Natalie was about to continue defending her staffing pattern, except she was interrupted by the surveyor.

Infection Control Interview

Natalie was extremely good at reining in her feelings, so with her face unreadable, she quietly backed off as the surveyor took the floor. Today of all days, the last thing she wanted was a flare up of her headache, so she had been proactive by taking her pain pills before leaving her office. Luckily it had started working.

"Thank you all for coming. I've been very impressed at the condition of your campus. I love the layout and the general condition in which it's kept. I must give credit to the Director of Environmental Services…" Ms. McNally consulted her sheet, trying to put a face with the name.

Not waiting for her to continue, Mr. Silvers, the director of Environmental Services, piped up, "Thank you Ms. McNally, but I can't take all the credit. Natalie and I've worked closely to establish the policies we have in place, so I have to give her and her department a lot of the credit."

Ms. McNally smiled. "That's very good to know, Mr. Silvers. Thank you."

She continued praising the hospital and the various departments she had visited. Finally, she looked at Natalie and smiled brightly.

"Natalie, why don't you tell me about your department? Everyone knows that Infection Control is one of the most essential departments in any hospital or healthcare facility. Based on the first standard, can you tell me what process you've been using to reduce the risks of nosocomial infections?" Ms. McNally asked.

Natalie smiled back. She then launched into a dissertation starting with the first IC standard.

"Well, on a daily basis, the first duty of the ICP is to review all new admissions and their room placements," Natalie began. "Based on the admitting diagnosis, they determine if additional review is necessary. If the patient has a history of a resistant organism, then it's a very good reason for additional review. They look at the current reason for admission, such as the presence of an elevated temperature or any wound drainage. If a draining wound is present, and a culture has been obtained, the preliminary result is reviewed. Depending on the result of these findings, the ICN will start a record on this patient, along with a note to visit this patient during rounds to determine appropriate placement. She will then notify the unit if this patient requires placement on 'contact precautions.' She will then inform... "

"Let me hear from one of your nurses," Ms. McNally turned and looked at each of the ICN's. You could literally see their hearts sinking into their shoes as they squirmed and tried to avoid making eye contact with the surveyor.

Candace was the first to recover. "Well, when a patient is placed on contact precautions, depending on the site of the infection, he or she will be placed in a single room with a sign placed on the door. Before entering that room, everyone will read the sign to determine what is needed before entering the room..."

"What about the family members? If I come to visit my loved one, and I see they're in a room with a sign on the door, I'm going to be very frightened. How are they informed? Let me hear from someone else." Ms. McNally looked at the ICN's again, and Rochelle picked up the dialogue.

"All nursing staff receives education about the different types of isolation precautions. It is part of their annual infection control mandatory training. They are also instructed on how to communicate with family members."

"What if they're not satisfied with the answers they're getting from the staff? Or what happens if the staff is unable to answer some of their questions. What then?" Ms. McNally asked.

"They're told to contact the ICN responsible for that unit. When we receive a call, we visit the unit and speak with the family members," responded Lisa.

"What if they still don't understand?" Ms. McNally asked. "Some people learn better visually. When there is something they can read at a later time, then they understand better..."

"That's not a problem. We have handouts for specific infections in terms that can be easily understood by most laypersons. So in addition to answering their questions face to face, we also provide them with educational material they can refer to later," Rochelle continued.

"This is a mixed community with people speaking many different languages. What about your patients and families who do not speak English?" Ms. McNally pressed.

"That has been taken care of. The pamphlets have been translated into the six languages most spoken in this area, which includes English, of course, Spanish, Italian, Russian, French, and Chinese," Kirsten jumped in.

"That's very good. I like that. Let's move on. How do you deal with exposures, especially to airborne organisms?" Ms. McNally asked.

Things were flowing smoothly. No one had messed up yet, and Natalie was smiling covertly as Lisa picked up the reins.

"When a patient comes into the emergency room and is suspected of having an airborne disease such as tuberculosis (TB), the doctors and nurses know that this patient will require airborne precautions. The first thing they will do is place that patient in a single room specially designed to prevent the air in that room from being disseminated to the outer corridor. It's what's referred to as a negative pressure room. All staff entering that room will need to wear personal protective equipment (PPE), which consists of specialized masks to prevent the inhalation of the TB bacilli."

"Can anyone wear those masks?" Ms. McNally asked.

"No. You have to be specially trained and fit tested before you are allowed to wear these masks," Lisa said.

"Why?" Ms. McNally asked.

"Well, if an employee has certain medical conditions such as asthma, this mask can make it difficult for them to breathe. The mask is designed to prevent inhaling the TB bacilli, so each employee has to be trained and receive a certificate stating they can wear this mask," Lisa said.

"Okay. So the patient is in the ER, but somehow no one suspects that he has TB. He goes to the unit, and after being in a room with another patient, the sputum that was taken while he was in the ER returns positive for acid-fast bacilli. What happens now?" Ms. McNally looked around the table, waiting for another ICN to pick up the ball. Her eyes landed and remained on Candace.

Candace had no choice; she picked up the ball and ran.

"Well, we are among the first to be notified by the TB lab, in addition to the patient's doctor. The unit where the patient is currently housed is also notified. We make sure that the patient is placed in a single room with negative pressure," Candace said.

"What if there are no negative pressure rooms?" Ms. McNally asked.

"We contact the Respiratory Care Department to provide a portable unit called a microcon unit. This unit has several layers of replaceable filters that trap the TB organism and clean and recirculate the air within the room. This unit is placed in the room, a sign stating, 'Airborne Precautions,' is placed on the door of the room, and the door is kept closed at all times. A cart containing all necessary supplies needed to enter that room is then placed outside the room. More often than not, a specially designed room is available. One important feature of this room is the anteroom. This is an area just before entering the room where the patient is housed," Candace said.

"Okay, what about the staff and other patients that have been exposed? Let me hear from someone else," Ms. McNally said.

Kirsten picked up the ball and ran.

"We then begin an investigation. This starts in the ER and then spreads out to all areas the patient might have visited, including the patient care unit. It is very labor intensive and takes a lot of time, sometimes many days.

"We obtain a list of all patients who were in the same room or area as the source patient. We collect the names of all staff who interacted with that patient without wearing the appropriate mask. We inform Occupational Health Services (OHS) that there has been an airborne exposure. The list of names is then submitted to OHS, and they retrieve the medical record of those employees…"

At this point, the surveyor realized the staff knew their jobs. She held up her hand, indicating she had heard all she needed to hear.

"Okay, you seem to have it all in place. I'm impressed." She looked at Natalie and smiled.

She looked around the table and settled on the Environmental Services representative.

"So tell me Mr. Silvers, what is your role in helping the Infection Control Department?"

The representative, who was one of the best looking, confident, and knowledgeable men around the table, smiled and jumped right in.

"Without our department doing its job correctly, there is no hospital. Our entire staff is trained by the infection control staff on the correct methods for cleaning all areas of the facility. The teaching is very, very specific. For example, the way an adult unit is cleaned is very different from the way the neonatal unit is cleaned. The staff is educated on the correct sequence for cleaning a unit. For example, when cleaning an area such as the operating room, the staff is instructed to work from a clean area to a dirty area, and when cleaning the walls, they start from the high area to the low.

"They're also taught how to properly dilute cleaning solutions so the efficacy is maintained. They also know how to correctly don, remove, and discard the appropriate protective garb to protect themselves from exposure to infectious agents. When cleaning an isolation room of a patient with a resistant organism such as *C. diff*, they know they must use a bleach solution diluted in a one to ten solution, rather than the regular cleaning solution," Mr. Silvers said.

"How do they know what organism this patient might have?" Ms. McNally asked.

"A list of patients on isolation is sent to us daily by the Infection Control Department. It contains the names of all patients on isolation, the rooms where they're isolated, and also the names of the organisms. Before my staff report to their assigned units, this list is reviewed with them. If they are unsure, or if they forget, they can always speak to the head nurse or call the Infection Control Department…" Mr. Silvers began picking up steam.

Realizing that the structure and the work the department had done was almost flawless, Ms. McNally decided to call a halt. "Thank you, Mr. Silvers," she said.

"Natalie, I've heard a lot today and I think that you have an excellent program in place. I guess I can now see a justification for your staffing." Ms. McNally smiled. "Are there additional projects or areas of interest you and your staff would like to share with me?"

"Yes, there are quite a number of areas. Let's start with education. We do massive staff education, because without knowledge, the employees are incapable of protecting themselves, their patients, and our visitors. So we work closely with the Nursing Education Department, and on a monthly basis, we are allotted two hours to educate the nursing staff.

"In addition, all department heads are aware that if they have a concern they can always request an in-service from us. To make it convenient, we will visit their department and work with small groups as much as possible. In fact, we encourage them to call. We are always available for consults. Any staff member can pick up a phone and call us with any infection control-related problem, and we assure them there are no stupid questions. All they have to do is call!" Natalie exclaimed.

The surveyor looked on in rapt attention as Natalie picked up speed.

"The ICN's tend to develop a good rapport with the staff on the units they're assigned to. So it's not unusual if they are sometimes called to the units to do in-services regarding specific issues, such as how to detect and report dangerous conditions during construction.

"The ICN's also keep track of culture results so they can determine when a patient needs to be removed from isolation…"

At this point, the surveyor interjected.

"Thank you, Natalie, I've heard enough. I'd like to hear from…" she looked around. "Dr. Corbin, chair of the Infection Control Committee. Am I right?"

"Yes you are," Dr. Corbin responded.

Infection Control Interview

By now, everyone at the table was relaxed because things continued to flow smoothly. However, it would have been unwise to become too complacent. All it would have taken was one incorrect response for things to become unglued and start snowballing.

Because the surveyor constantly took notes during the interview process, it made it easy for her to consult her notes at the end of a session and request a policy to validate a previous response. So far, however, there had been no gaffs, and everyone had hoped this trend would continue.

"Dr. Corbin, can you describe your role in the Infection Control Department? What is your function?" Ms. McNally asked.

"Infectious disease has always been my passion, and as you know, I do consultation on patients throughout the facility who are suspected of having infections. I'm also in charge of the Infectious Disease Clinic here on site. I meet with Natalie and the infection control team monthly or as needed to discuss practices, any issues with specific departments, or patient placement. The team keeps me updated on the patients who are in isolation, and if there is an issue regarding an exposure, I'm informed. I also meet with the team monthly or as needed to discuss blood stream infections and other infections that are being tracked for reporting to the CDC and at the Infection Control Committee meeting," Dr. Corbin said.

"How often do you hold your committee meetings?" Ms. McNally asked.

"We have those monthly."

"You are aware that you do not have to hold your meetings that frequently?"

"Yes, we are aware of the policy change, however the decision was made to continue meeting monthly. This allows us to stay on track so that any issues arising can be addressed on a timely basis and not fall through the cracks. So overall, everyone benefits."

"Okay, thank you Dr. Corbin," Ms. McNally said.

The interview continued along the same vein, addressing representatives from the other departments.

· · ·

The pharmacy representative was the next member chosen, and everyone knew him to be intensely intellectual with a wild sense of humor. He had been encouraged to tone down his sense of humor during the conference, but no one knew for sure what to expect.

"I'd like to hear from the pharmacy representative," said the surveyor, looking around the table.

A lanky olive complexioned African American with a head full of shocking red hair piped up. "I'm Harold Burke, and I represent the Pharmacy. Everyone calls me Harry," he said.

A huge, goofy smile covered his handsome face as he looked at the surveyor. Every head at the table turned and focused on Harry, each holding their breath, wondering if this was going to be the end of what had so far been a successful interview process.

Ms. McNally smiled as she looked at the quirky looking pharmacist.

"Okay, Harry. What's your role in Infection Control? What do you contribute in terms of helping to save patients' lives?" she asked.

Harry had the floor. He was very cerebral, and this was his opportunity to espouse a subject that was near and dear to his heart.

"Well, Ms. McNally, I love my job, and I believe I was born to do what I do," Harry said.

Everyone at the table rolled their eyes and bit their lips to keep from laughing out loud. Ms. McNally smiled as he continued.

"My job consists of monitoring patients who are receiving multiple antibiotics. My job is to ensure that these antibiotics are working in sync with each other. I'm also responsible for ensuring that the prescribed antibiotics are working effectively and don't compromise the functions of important organs such as the liver and kidneys. I work closely with the doctors. Dr. Corbin can attest to this." At this point, Harry turned to look at Dr. Corbin who smiled and nodded. He paused.

"I monitor prescribed physician orders to ensure that a patient is not being given an antibiotic after it's no longer needed, based on culture reports. My job is to work in tandem with the doctors and act as another eye for them to ensure that patients receive only the medication they absolutely need. Now I'm not a doctor, but if I can help to prevent one patient from dying, then I believe I'm doing a good job," Harry said.

Ms. McNally started clapping followed by everyone at the table. "Thank you, Harry. I think that is just wonderful."

A huge sigh of relief was audible around the table, everyone realizing that Harry had not ruined the interview process. Consulting her notes, the surveyor moved on to the bacteriology lab representative.

• • •

Frances Malloy had been through the JCAHO process several times, so this was familiar territory. If she felt any fear or anxiety, it was certainly not reflected in her voice or in her demeanor as she stated her role.

"My role is to inform the various departments when a resistant organism is identified. These include the doctor caring for the patient, the Infection Control Department, and the unit where the patient is housed. Timely notification of the respective departments is extremely important in order to prevent an exposure or avoid delay of appropriate treatment," Francis said.

"What is the most prevalent organism identified in your lab? Correct me if I'm wrong, but it's my understanding that there are some that are more prevalent in your community?" asked the surveyor.

"Yes," replied Francis. "Recently there has been a large influx of community acquired MRSA. Just recently a new policy of obtaining cultures was implemented, so we are receiving a lot more specimens than previously."

"Has your staff been increased to handle this increased number of specimens?" Ms. McNally asked.

Francis smiled as she replied, "Not to date, but I've been promised that I'll be receiving additional staff soon."

"Well, let's hope that happens soon," replied Ms. McNally.

• • •

Glancing at her watch, Natalie realized they had almost finished the allotted time scheduled for the interview, and there were still some other areas that had not yet been interviewed. However, the surveyor did not seem to be in any hurry, so the only option for everyone was to go with the flow.

The Respiratory Care Department was next in line, and the representative was a veteran in his field and very professional, both in demeanor and knowledge.

"And let me hear from you Mr. . ." Ms. McNally glanced at her notes.

"Lucas," he interjected.

"Mr. Lucas, thank you. Why don't you tell me about your role in Infection Control?"

"First, let me start by saying that the respiratory care staff and Natalie and her staff have a very close working relationship. The staff in my department receives infection control education annually, and we're in constant communication as needed.

"We are responsible for care and maintenance of all the mechanical ventilators used between patients. My staff is knowledgeable about how to appropriately dispose of all respiratory equipment in the specially designed red containers known as regulated medical waste or RMW containers.

"We work with these portable units known as microcons that are used on patients with tuberculosis or suspected of having tuberculosis. It's important that the filters in these units are changed at the appropriate intervals based on the manufacturers' recommendations..."

"Could you tell me a bit more about these units? I have heard them mentioned more than once today, but I've never heard of them before. Can you please explain how these are cleaned?" asked Ms. McNally.

"Oh yes, of course," Mr. Lucas said. "Depending on the number of patients on airborne isolation, there may be a shortage of negative pressure rooms. When this occurs, a suspected patient is placed in a single room, and nursing informs us that they need a microcon unit. It's the responsibility of our department to supply these units and ensure that they're clean and functioning adequately. When the isolation orders are discontinued, nursing will inform my department. We then retrieve the unit and make sure it's cleaned and serviced in time for use when it's needed again.

"Cleaning is done using a one in ten bleach solution. Each unit is numbered, and a log is maintained by the department. The appropriate personal protective equipment is utilized when cleaning and disposing of the soiled filters in order to prevent transmission of infectious organisms," Mr. Lucas said.

By now, everyone was desperately trying to disguise the fatigue they were feeling and hoping that the end would soon be in sight.

The surveyor looked around the table and sighed.

"Ladies and gentlemen, I know I'm going a bit beyond the time allotted, but this has been such an interesting group. I feel reluctant to end this interview. However, if you would just bear with me, as soon as I hear from the Dietary Department, I'll let you be on your way," Ms. McNally said.

Everyone around the table took a deep breath and tried calling on their energy reserves.

"This lady doesn't know when to call it quits," Candace whispered to Lisa.

"I know," Lisa whispered back, kicking Candace under the table.

Happy to hear that the end was now in sight, Ebony from the Dietary Department quickly jumped in.

"I'm Ebony Mahoney from Food and Nutrition. My department also works very closely with Infection Control. We're aware that food borne illnesses can be fatal, so we work hard to ensure cleanliness of the food preparation areas. We have designated food prep areas, with separate areas being used specifically for meat prep. There are sinks designated for hand washing away from the food prep areas to prevent food contamination. It's important that the water be kept at the correct temperature for cleaning and sanitizing utensils and that hot foods are kept hot and cold foods kept cold."

"What happens if your staff gets ill, do you allow them to keep working, or is there a policy for treating them?" asked Ms. McNulty.

"The staff has been educated about the importance of being healthy and free from communicable diseases when working in the department. They are aware that if they have any open wounds, boils or rashes, they must report to OHS. They're also aware that they can't report to work until they receive medical clearance from OHS. And finally, they've been educated about the importance of keeping scheduled appointments with OHS for annual physical assessment as per hospital policy," Ebony said.

"I'm really pleased at this presentation and impressed by how you all seem to work together as a team. I wish I could see that in more of the hospitals I visit," Ms. McNally said.

She smiled as everyone basked in the good vibrations her words were creating.

Looking around the table, she continued, "You have truly demonstrated an excellent example of good team work, and I'll make sure that this is reflected in the final evaluation. Thank you, everyone, and continue the good work."

As she was escorted from the room, smiles broke out on the faces of every team member. Conversations picked up in several small groups as each person prepared to exit the room, each realizing they could now breathe just a little bit easier.

However, it was not yet the end.

JCAHO Summation 44

Although this was the last interview of the survey process, the work of the surveyors was not yet finished. They spent at least an hour and a half to preparing their preliminary report before they left the facility. This report contained all their observations, plus a preliminary accreditation decision.

As everyone returned to their respective work area, the number one thought on everyone's mind was that crucial phone call that summoned a return to the conference room for the summation conference.

Throughout the entire survey process, this was the only time the conference room would be open to employees other than specific department heads and the management team. Other employees, such as head nurses and supervisors, were welcomed to the summation. After weeks of preparation, the primary thought on everyone's mind was the outcome following all the hard work.

Finally the call came!

As many employees as the conference room could contain crammed into the space, ready to receive the news, good or bad.

For the next thirty minutes, Mr. Saunders received the exit briefing and the atmosphere was tense as every ear tuned in to the words of the chief surveyor.

First the standards were reviewed, followed by the compliance issues. The report of the outcome of their week's survey was finally revealed. Mr. Saunders received a written preliminary accreditation decision report, along with a "Summary of Survey Findings Report." This report informed the facility to identify any requirement for improvements that might be needed.

At last the surveyors prepared to exit the facility.

For the time being, based on the preliminary report, the facility had been granted full accreditation!

A cheer went up from the crowd, but was quickly brought under control by a raised hand from Mr. Saunders.

"I would like to thank everyone for their hard work in getting us through this process. We would like to show our appreciation by inviting everyone to join us in the cafeteria for some refreshments," he said.

The final accreditation decision for the organization, which was valid for approximately three years, had yet to be awarded in one of a number of categories. But for now, the burden had been lifted, and the administrator would anxiously await the arrival of the official written report. He would then proudly display the plaque in a prominent place, announcing to the entire world that Justice Medical Center is JCAHO accredited.

Everyone exited the room and headed for the cafeteria, where a sumptuous feast has been prepared.

If administration failed to show their feelings for their employees the rest of the year, there was no lack of them during survey time. Mr. Saunders was the first to get the celebration started. He did this in his usual flamboyant style by giving a rousing speech, which included liberal thanks and praise to the entire hospital staff. This was followed by Chief Nurse Executive Samantha Brown, who thanked the entire nursing staff, giving special mention to the different teams responsible for record review.

There was eating, music, laughter, and great camaraderie. Even the stuffed shirts were schmoozing with the little people, shaking hands, rubbing shoulders, and thanking them for their hard work preparing for the survey.

After a while, the satiated ones slowly make their way back to their work areas so others could come and partake in the festivities. Time slipped by, but very few took notice. Everyone was in full celebration mode. The music was still good, and the food was still hot, and still the partying continued until well after dark.

Samantha Brown 45

Samantha had been doing her best to fit in and be productive in her new position. She tried hard not to rock the boat and to remain as obscure as possible while picking the brains of everyone around her. There was no love lost between Natalie and her, but Natalie was trying to dig deep within herself to find what it took to remain civil toward Samantha.

Natalie had met with her a few times after the *C. diff* scare, but Samantha, realizing Natalie was no match for her, had given up her little game.

The post-JCAHO celebration was in full swing, and everyone's mood was waxing mellow when Samantha spotted Natalie and her staff entering the cafeteria.

Samantha gingerly made her way toward Natalie with arms outstretched, wobbling on her six-inch heels. Between trying to maintain her balance and holding onto her cup to prevent her drink from spilling, she presented quite a picture.

Samantha greeted Natalie like a long-lost friend. Voice dripping with honey, she held out both arms in anticipation of a hug.

"Natalie! How good to see you here. I'm so proud of how well your department performed," Samantha said.

Natalie plastered a smile on her face, while managing to sidestep the outstretched tentacles.

"Hi, Samantha, it's nice to see you too. Thanks for the compliment, and yes, my staff does work extremely hard. There is never a dull moment in our department," Natalie said.

"Natalie, I really had no idea Infection Control was so complex. Now that JCAHO is behind us, I would love to meet with you to learn more about what you do. It seems like a really interesting area, and I think I could learn a lot from you. So can we schedule a time to meet? I'll come up to your office. This way, I won't be disturbed with constant pesky phone calls," Samantha said.

As if I don't get phone calls too, Natalie thought to herself.

Trying hard to keep smiling, Natalie replied, "Why don't you have your secretary call my secretary and set up a time? Claudine will gladly take care of it."

I must remember to tell Claudine not to schedule any meeting with Samantha for the next few week, or months, if possible, Natalie told herself while giving Samantha her most intriguing smile.

"Good. That sounds like a plan. See you soon," Samantha said.

Spotting other cohorts across the room, Samantha hurriedly took off to continue her marathon of hugging, kissing, and laughing.

Natalie Sinclair 46

JCAHO was now old news, and it was time for Natalie to finally face her fears. A part of her wanted to know the cause of her headaches and another part feared knowing. She had always believed that *knowledge is power*, but she now realized that when it came to her personal self, that knowledge was just too painful to face.

She had an appointment at Kendall Medical for an MRI with contrast the following day and already her anxiety level had started a slow, steady climb. She would have liked to cancel, but Steve would not hear of it, and deep down the rational side of her totally agreed with him.

Luckily, the day had been going well so far, and hopefully it would continue in that vein. There were no meetings scheduled, and the staff was doing their best to catch up on their reports and doing the myriad of other things that were required from the Infection Control Department. Candace would be in charge while Natalie had the day off to keep her MRI appointment.

Unfortunately, the day for the MRI did not start out well. From the moment Steve entered the main highway, traffic was at a standstill. The radio station they were listening to did not report any accidents, disabled vehicles, or work zone issues ahead. The highway was the most direct route to the medical center and using a different highway had just never entered Steve's mind.

After spending an hour and a half on the highway, a trip that normally took a third of the time, they finally arrived. Steve had called ahead, and his secretary had informed the MRI Department that Natalie would be late. They went directly to the MRI Department, and the staff wasted no time getting things started.

Natalie completed the required consent form, which included the "Patient Screening Form for Contrast." This was reviewed by the nurse, then the radiologist, who made sure that everything was in order. The supervising physician was present in the MRI suite just in case of any emergencies, and Natalie felt much more secure knowing he was close by.

As she lay on the table patiently waiting, he walked over and introduced himself.

"Hi, Natalie. I'm Dr. Stewart. I know your husband Steve. We've worked together many times." He took her hands and squeezed them reassuringly.

"You're in good hands. Just try and relax. Do you have any questions?" Dr. Stewart asked.

"No. I'm fine." Natalie replied.

"Okay. We'll be getting started shortly."

Dr. Stewart turned and left the room, leaving Natalie feeling a lot more reassured.

She knew she would be receiving the contrast media via the intravenous route, so she rolled up her sleeves so the technician could locate a vein. She was not afraid of needles, but she was also not a fan.

After introducing herself and explaining the procedure, the nurse applied a rubber tourniquet to Natalie's left upper arm and tightened it in place.

She smiled at Natalie, "Can you make a fist please?"

Natalie complied, and a vein became clearly visible in the depression at the inner aspect of the elbow, known as the antecubital fossa. The nurse quickly swabbed the area with an alcohol swab, followed by another clean dry swab. In no time, a large bore twenty-gauge needle was inserted. A flash of blood appeared in the clear plastic cannula, and withdrawing a small sample of blood quickly identified venous backflow. A peripheral intravenous line was then attached.

"That wasn't too bad, was it?" asked the nurse.

"No," Natalie replied. "I barely felt it."

After attaching a plastic intravenous tubing, the nurse checked the patency of the catheter by flushing it with a small amount of 0.9% normal saline. No resistance, pain, or swelling was encountered, so she secured the catheter in place and exited the room.

The technician then entered, identified himself, and attached the syringe containing the contrast media to the hub of the IV line and very slowly injected the contrast media.

As the media entered her vein, Natalie felt a slight tingling sensation accompanied by a feeling of warmth all over as the solution travelled up her vein. However, she was not too worried. She knew this feeling was not unusual, having done her research ahead of time. She also knew that there was a cart available nearby containing emergency supplies in the event any adverse reactions should they occur.

Hopefully it would not be needed today.

Soon the scan was in progress, and Natalie was trying her hardest to relax, wishing that it was over and that the results showed that everything was okay.

Her wish was soon granted, as the technician and the nurse soon reentered the room.

"All finished, Ms. Sinclair. How are you feeling?" the technician asked.

"I feel a bit warm," she replied fanning herself. "I also feel a bit light-headed."

"That will pass in a little while. I'm going to let the IV solution run for a while before removing the catheter."

After about a half-hour, the nurse returned and flushed the catheter with 10cc of 0.9% normal saline. The tubing was disconnected, and the IV site was inspected for any swelling or indication of extravasation, or migration of the solution into the tissues. The nurse inspected the site, which appeared free from any signs of complications, so a small dressing was applied, and a pamphlet with post-MRI instructions was given to Natalie.

Steve had cancelled his remaining appointments for the day and was anxiously waiting for Natalie. As she left the scan room, he met her at the door.

He gave her a quick hug. "How are you feeling?" he asked anxiously.

"Tired and hungry," Natalie replied.

"Me too. Let's go find some food," Steve said.

They held hands tightly as they headed for the elevator, then out the door to the parking lot.

"Where are we going?" Natalie asked, thinking they were going to the cafeteria.

"I'm off the rest of the day. I have a surprise for you," Steve said.

"This had better be a great surprise. I think I'm going to pass out before I get there," Natalie said.

They got into his car and headed north. The landscape flew by and soon Natalie was staring at the most beautiful edifice she had ever seen.

She gazed on in awe. "What is this place?" she asked.

Quick as a flash, the valet materialized, held her door open, and whisked away the car.

Steve smiled at her look of wonderment. "This is a new restaurant. It opened less than a month ago. I met the owner when I fixed his leg. He broke it in a skiing accident. He thinks he owes me, so I'm here to collect."

They were greeted warmly in person by the owner as they entered. He seated them at a corner table where the view was just to die for.

They enjoyed a sumptuous meal, and before long, they were on their way home to anxiously await the news that could mean a big change in both their lives.

Brandon Saunders 47

No one was happier to see the end of JCAHO than Brandon. He had kept his feelings regarding his blackmailer carefully guarded during the entire survey process, and he made sure he did not miss a single dose of his medicine. However, there were times when he felt like he was wound so tight, he might just spontaneously combust.

However, this was a new week and a new day, and he was going to take care of that little punk who was trying to ruin his life, once and for all.

On his way to work, he decided to stop by the local bank. He placed a call to Laura his secretary to let her know he would be late. He was well known at the bank, and immediately when he entered, he was greeted by name by one of the bank managers.

"Hi, Mr. Saunders. How can we help you today?" the manager asked.

Brandon smiled back. "I just need to get something from my safety deposit box."

Mr. Stark, the senior bank official, escorted him one flight down to the deposit vault. After greeting the armed security guard seated at the entrance to the vault, the manager made sure he located Brandon's security box, and then left him to conduct his business in private.

Brandon would not admit it to anyone, but whenever he entered the vault, an intense feeling of claustrophobia always overcame him. The massive stainless steel doors appeared to be no less than three or four feet in thickness and he could not imagine anyone being locked in one of those things. The entire room seemed just too intimidating; it always gave him the creeps. He shook off his morbid thoughts and steeled himself to pay attention to the business at hand.

"I'm here on a mission. The sooner I get it accomplished, the sooner I can get out of this place," he said.

Brandon removed the metal box and carefully placed it on the table. Inside the box were three large envelopes that he also placed on the table. He then returned the metal box to its original location before turning his attention to the envelopes. Next he removed the contents of two of the envelopes: four bundles of large denomination bills held together by large rubber bands. The total amount was two hundred thousand dollars. He carefully placed the four bundles in his briefcase. Last, but not least, he turned his attention to the third envelope. His hands were getting clammy as he removed the contents. As he gazed down at the object in his hand he could not help but feel how cold, hard, and lifeless it felt to his touch.

"Steel is so cold, just like death," he said softly, as he cradled the .45 mm handgun in his hands. After making sure there was a bullet in each chamber, he placed it gently into his briefcase alongside the four bundles of cash.

He smiled at the guard as he exited the vault. "Have a nice day, Bernie. I plan on having a great one myself."

The guard looked up in surprise from the magazine he was reading.

"Goodbye, Mr. Saunders." Bernie said. "I didn't even know he knew my name," he said to himself, staring at Brandon's back as Mr. Stark escorted him out the door.

As Brandon hurried to his car, he wondered how the day would end. But before he started thinking too deeply, he decided to get himself some breakfast.

"I know how this will end. This is my show," he said to himself as he entered the doors to his favorite diner.

He was well known at this diner. The waitresses liked his friendly demeanor, and they all wanted him seated at their table. For one thing, he was a man that enjoyed his food, and most of all he was a very generous tipper.

"Hi, Mr. Saunders," Dolly called out as he walked to a vacant table.

"Hi, Dolly. I'll have the usual please," Brandon said.

No sooner than he was seated, a well-stacked plate of pancakes, scrambled eggs, bacon, and home fries was placed before him, followed by a full beaker of coffee.

"This looks good, Dolly. You know just the way I like it," Brandon said.

"Well, I've been serving you a long time. I know what you like," she said suggestively.

Brandon chose to ignore the come-on and delved into his food. He ate like he had not eaten in a long time, savoring every mouthful, and smiling as he thought about his appointment later.

He was meeting with his unknown "friend" after work and anything was possible. He had finally broken down and consented to meet with him after receiving several phone calls at work. The final call had really scared him to the point he knew he had to stop this person.

Laura, his secretary, greeted him with a smile as he entered the office.

"Good morning, Mr. Saunders, or should I say good afternoon?" she asked.

Brandon kept walking, his back to Laura. She knew he was smiling, but Brandon always knew he was the boss, and Laura knew just how far she could go without actually crossing the line.

She followed him to his office and peeked inside. "You had a call from Dr. Sam. There's a meeting scheduled for one o'clock, in his office," she said.

"Did he say what's it about?" Brandon asked.

"No, but…"

"Well, am I supposed to just show up unprepared? Laura, do you want me looking like a fool in front of the medical director?"

Laura crossed her arms over her chest, her feet tapping as she smiled.

"Relax, Mr. Saunders. He's just having a get together for department heads to say thanks for JCAHO."

Brandon's face relaxed as he breathed a sigh of relief.

"Laura, if you weren't my secretary for all these years, I'd fire you."

Laura smiled in return. "Oh no you would not, I know too many of your secrets," she said to herself.

Dr. Samuel Ashman

Dr. Samuel Ashman had been the medical director at Justice for the past fifteen years. Under his leadership, the medical program had flourished and had produced thousands of young, talented doctors in various areas of specializations.

The Residency Program was known far and wide for its diversity. At the end of the program, some residents had chosen to follow their residency with a fellowship, while others were eagerly snatched up to staff other medical centers and universities. Some chose to go into successful private practices.

Dr. Sam was an imposing figure, tall and muscular with a great sense of humor. His favorite joke was about his hair or lack thereof. To know him was to love him, and he was loved by almost everyone. He never forgot a face or a name, and his signature greeting was, "Call me, Dr. Sam."

He had been born in Manchester, England and had come to the States with his parents and sister when he was only ten. He was now sixty years old, but still had some residue of that beautiful British accent. Although he was a loving person, when it came to business, especially the business of Justice, he could be tough as nails.

By one o'clock all of upper management was gathered in Dr. Sam's office, shaking hands, slapping backs, and smiling at each other. For the moment any ill will was left at the door, forgotten for the moment, to be resurrected at a later date and time.

Dr. Sam started the celebration by hoisting his flute of sparkling apple cider and offering a toast to those assembled.

"Thank you all for coming. Let me start by giving a big thank you for all your hard work in preparation for JCAHO. It is because of your hard work that we have been awarded another three-year accreditation."

A round of applause broke out, but he had just started, so he held up his hand for silence. "Please hold your applause," he begged.

"I appreciate, as always, everyone going the extra mile, postponing your plans, and some of you even ignoring your families to stay late and allowing this to happen. Let us continue to keep our vision simple yet goal focused, remembering that all our efforts and all that we do we do for our patients. Without our patients, there is no us. So let us continue to work hard and create a vision whereby our name becomes synonymous with excellence and outstanding quality and service. So please raise your glasses and drink to the continued prosperity of Justice Medical Center. Thank you," Dr. Sam said.

A deafening applause was again brought under control as he raised his hands. "Let's eat, everybody," he said.

Lobster, caviar, and sparkling cider flowed in abundance, though alcohol was strictly forbidden.

Natalie Sinclair

At last the long awaited call came. David wanted to meet with Steve and Natalie on Wednesday to discuss the results of her brain MRI. Her headaches had gotten more intense and required her to take more of her pain medication. Her vision had become quite blurry, and sometimes she had difficulty with her peripheral vision. She had also found herself leaning against objects for support, because more and more, she experienced difficulty with her balance.

All this she kept to herself as she did not want to worry Steve, and most of all, she did not want sympathy from her staff.

Luckily she still had the car service, so she was able to take a short nap on her way to and sometimes from work. At first she had been annoyed at what she had thought of as interference on Steve's part by providing the car service. However, her feelings had completely changed, and she now felt she would be forever grateful to Steve for his thoughtfulness and frequently expressed her thanks.

The appointment with David was scheduled for nine o'clock on Wednesday, and Steve and Natalie were present and on time to receive the news, good or bad.

They met David in his office, and once again Natalie was very impressed with the comfortable chairs. She even took time to absorb the tasteful but masculine decor of his office. They greeted each other and David tried some easy conversation to set Natalie's mind at ease. Finally he decided to deliver the news, as difficult as it was.

"Steve, Natalie, I'm going to get right to the point. I met with Dr. Stewart and reviewed your MRI in its entirety, and I really wish I had better news. Steve, you know Dr. Stewart, he's very experienced and thorough, and I trust him completely. I'll let you both see the films so you can both get an idea of what I'm talking about."

Steve nodded in response as David walked over to the other side of the room and flipped a switch. The old-fashioned X-ray light-box mounted on the wall flickered as the fluorescent bulbs came to life then stabilized. He switched off the overhead lights, then moved toward the light-box and slipped two films into the mounted light-box. These films were available on his desktop computer, but he wanted both Steve and Natalie to view the films for themselves, so he chose to use the old-fashioned x-ray light box.

A large area on the left side of Natalie's MRI lit up like a Christmas tree. Steve started in surprise as the image sprang to life. He was unsure of what he was seeing, but he instinctively knew something was wrong.

In normal MRI scans, the left and right sides of the brains are almost always similar in size. If there is a major difference in size between some parts of the brain, it is usually a sign of an abnormal finding. Most illnesses or disorders affect only a very small part of the brain, so it is common to have normal images in most areas and abnormal findings in small areas only.

As David continued his review of the MRI, both Steve and Natalie's anxiety level continued to rise. However, he wanted to be open and honest with them, so he delivered the news the best way he knew how.

He pointed to an area on the film that showed one large mass with a cluster of smaller masses in the parietal lobe.

"Both Dr. Stewart and I agree that this appears to be a glioma. The lesions appear to be in the area that controls vision, along with other senses. What we would like to do—without delay— is a biopsy to confirm this diagnosis. This will also differentiate the tumor from other type of masses."

This was not the first time Natalie had received bad news, but it had never impacted her directly. This time it was different. This was like being hit with a thunderbolt. For a while it seemed as though she was having an out-of-body experience. She attempted to speak, but the words seemed to stick in her throat.

Steve stared at her, worried that she might be having another seizure. He nudged her. She shook her head appearing startled.

"Honey, are you okay?" Steve asked.

She shook her head. "I really don't know."

"Do you have any questions for David?"

Natalie shook her head no.

This was so unlike her, but under the circumstances, it was totally understandable. Steve decided to ask a question. At least she would still be able to hear David's explanation. Whether she would be able to absorb it was another matter altogether.

"David, could you explain gliomas? What they are, how they present, and what is the prognosis."

"Well, as you know, gliomas are the most common of the primary malignant brain tumors. They're usually highly invasive and very disabling, and the prognosis tends to be very poor. They tend to be primary, and start in the brain. However, they don't spread to other body sites. The difficulty with gliomas is that there are no clear boundaries between the tumor and the healthy tissue. This usually makes surgical resection very difficult."

David's attention was focused on Natalie. She was not making eye contact, but her feelings were continuously playing themselves on her face.

David finished off his discussion by scheduling a date for Natalie's biopsy. He felt wretched and miserable for delivering such terrible news. After all, these were very nice people. They were in the healing arts just like he was, doing good wherever they could.

Why did nature have to be so cruel?

Brandon Saunders

Brandon was on pins and needles the entire day. He could barely contain himself as the hands of the clock kept creeping like a snail toward 5:00. At one point, he forced himself to tear his eyes away from the clock and do some meaningful work.

He smiled to himself as another one of his mother's little sayings came to mind: "A watched pot never boils." However, this certainly did not deter him in any way from his clock watching.

Finally it was five o'clock. Brandon grabbed his briefcase and headed out to Maroni's, determined to reclaim his life. This was his first visit to the restaurant and it took a while for his eyes to adjust to the dim lighting. All around him was a sea of people, each one trying to shout louder than the other in order to be heard. He realized he would have to fight his way inside. He elbowed his way toward the rear, searching for an empty table. At the same time he kept wondering if his "friend" was already waiting or if he had to hang around and wait. He was certainly in no mood for waiting this evening.

"Don't these people ever go home?" he asked himself.

As his eyes adjusted to the dark, he searched the crowd for his friend. He had no idea what he looked like, but it certainly did not hurt to look. Brandon certainly was not expecting someone with the word "blackmailer" written on his forehead, but one just never knew. He ordered a beer, and took his time savoring it. He saw some familiar faces, but did not know them personally, so he tried his best not to make eye contact. He finished his beer and was about to order another when his cell phone rang. He fished it out of the side pocket of his coat and glanced at the screen. He did not recognize the caller, but decided to answer it anyway.

"Who is this?" he asked.

"Hey, Brandon, this is your friend. I'm sorry I'm running a bit late, but I'll be there in another fifteen minutes. Don't leave."

"I'm not going to waste my time…"

The line went dead. Brandon angrily clicked off and returned the phone to his pocket.

He sat drumming his fingers on the table, debating his next move. He did not have long to wait.

Pushing his way through the crowd a skinny dark complexioned young man approached his table. Without saying a word, he made himself comfortable at the table and stared at Brandon. Brandon did not recognize him and was about to tell him he was holding the seat for someone. However, those dark, piercing eyes had him mesmerized.

Before he got the chance to speak, his new companion asked, "Hi, Brandon. Remember me?"

Brandon stared, trying to recall where he had seen this face. His heart was starting to pound, as he tried hard to recall the face. He swallowed hard.

"No, I don't. Why don't you refresh my memory?" Brandon said.

His friend smiled, showing his dirty, unkempt teeth. There were gaps where some teeth were missing, and Brandon tried his best not to stare.

"Before we get reacquainted, why don't you buy me a drink?" he said.

Against his better judgment, Brandon asked, "What would you like?"

"I only drink Budweiser. Don't you know it's the king of beers?" he said smiling with his missing teeth. Brandon signaled for a waiter and ordered the beer. His new friend took a deep drink, swallowed noisily as he leaned back against the chair, acting as though he had all the time in the world.

Brandon was getting impatient. He wanted to get this business over and done with. He knew this was the hangout for a lot of employees from Justice, and he definitely did not want to be seen with this character. He was not sure how he would explain his relationship with someone looking the way he did.

"So are you going to tell me your name?" asked Brandon impatiently.

"Don't lose your cool, Brandon. You've always had a short fuse, and I can see that hasn't changed one bit. Anyway, my name is Rajah," he said. He had a mild trace of a South Asian accent. "Does that ring a bell?"

Brandon's mind did a quick flashback as his eyes opened wide.

It all started coming back.

"You were part of that Indian family that lived down the hall," the words tumbled from Brandon's lips.

"Yes, I am. I'm glad your memory's coming back. That's very good. Do you remember when we were kids?" he smiled and paused as his mind went back to his childhood.

A light ignited in Brandon's eyes. He became speechless as his mind went back to the days when he lived in the projects.

As a small boy, he was thought of as just a high-strung kid, but as he entered his teens, everyone realized it was much more than that.

It all came to a head one day when he flew into a rage and completely thrashed his parents' apartment. He was uncontrollable and could not be restrained. In the process of this uncontrolled rampage, Brandon's parents had been injured, requiring a visit to the emergency room for multiple stitches. That's when the men in the white suits came to take him away.

His mother had cried and begged for them not to take him away.

"He's a good boy," she cried. "He just made a mistake."

But they refused to listen.

Brandon remembered the faces of all the neighbors crowding and staring as he was taken away crying and screaming.

He was hospitalized for six months and diagnosed with bipolar disorder. Three successive hospitalizations accompanied by numerous psychotherapy sessions and medications had finally made him into a new person.

After the final hospital admission, followed by numerous out-patient therapy sessions, his condition had stabilized. He had then followed his dream and enrolled in a local college. It took years of constant struggle, but Brandon had clung to his dreams and had graduated with a degree in hospital administration.

Brandon Saunders

Seeing Rajah brought back so many bad memories. Brandon was determined not to go back to the past. He was finished with it, so he shook himself back to the present and faced his nemesis.

"So do you have my money?" asked Rajah.

"Yes, I do, but what's the hurry? Tell me about yourself. What have you been doing with your life?"

"I don't want to talk about that," replied Rajah angrily. "I can see life has been very good with you, so let's just get down to business, and then we can both go our separate ways."

"If I give you what you want, how do I know you won't be back for more?" asked Brandon.

"You'll never know, now will you?" Rajah replied smiling.

An uncomfortable silence settled between them.

Suddenly Brandon decided he did not want to spend another second with Rajah.

"Let's get this over. I have your money, but I don't want to do business here. Can we go someplace where it's quiet, where we won't be noticed?" Brandon asked.

"Sure, I know just the place. Follow me," Rajah said.

Rajah drained the last of his beer and headed out the door, expecting Brandon to follow. Brandon lagged behind, just in case anyone recognized him; he did not want it to appear as if they were together. Rajah headed out the door toward an alleyway between two apartment buildings. It appeared dark and deserted, even though it was still a bit light out. For a minute Brandon thought about turning and running. Not that he would make it very far; considering the shape he was in, he was no match for Rajah.

For the longest time, he had been planning to go to the gym but had never seemed to make the time. *As soon as this is over, my first priority will be going to the gym to get myself in shape*, he promised himself.

He trudged on behind Rajah, wondering how far he was planning on taking him. It was really getting creepy now, and he wanted to get this over.

"How much further?" Brandon asked angrily.

"This will do," Rajah called out. "No one can see us here."

Brandon was about five yards behind him.

"Okay, let me have it," Rajah called out, hands outstretched.

"Come and get it," Brandon replied.

As Rajah started walking towards him, Brandon reached into his briefcase. Instead of reaching for the money, he came up with a gun. He pointed it at Rajah's chest.

Fear washed over Rajah's face as he saw the gun, but he tried to pass it off with feigned bravado.

"You won't shoot me," he laughed nervously. "What about your fancy job? They won't want a murderer working for them. Go ahead, shoot me!" he opened his arms wide as he advanced toward Brandon.

Brandon fired twice. Rajah fell backward, eyes opened wide in surprise. He attempted to get up, but only succeeded in flopping onto his side. Blood spurted from the opening in his chest, and slowly spread over his shirt, pooling under his right side.

With adrenaline coursing through his veins, Brandon walked over to the body and pushed it with his foot. He looked at it closely, observing only a slight rise and fall of his chest.

"You think you can just appear out of thin air and demand my money?" he asked angrily. "I don't think so. I've worked way too hard for this."

Brandon raised the gun and shot Rajah in the head twice more for good measure.

Brandon looked both ways, and then picked up his briefcase and the money that had fallen out, pocketed the gun and hurried out of the alley. He reached his car, settled in, and quickly closed and locked the door.

As he hurriedly backed out of the parking space, the rear bumper of his Benz collided with the front bumper of a white Toyota parked behind him. The impact threw his head back connecting it with the headrest, causing him to grab on to his neck as pain shot up the back of his head. He recovered quickly and peeled out of the spot, tires squealing. As he entered the highway, he encountered the worst traffic jam ever.

"Everyone and their mother seems to be heading home from work at the same time tonight," Brandon mumbled.

As he sat in traffic, he wondered if there had been any serious damage done to his precious Benz.

It took him two hours to get to his condominium.

• • •

Entering the underground parking for his condo, he headed for his assigned space.

"This has been the worst day of my life," he said to himself as he extricated himself from behind the steering wheel. He walked around to the rear. He could not believe his eyes.

The bumper was barely held in place by a few small pieces of wire. It was a miracle that it had stayed attached all the way home. Anger washed over him as he looked at his prized possession.

I'm glad he's dead. If he weren't, I'd find him and kill him, Brandon thought to himself, placing the blame squarely on Rajah.

He had his mechanic on speed dial, so he hurriedly pulled out his cell phone and placed a call. As the phone rang, he started sweating. Finally the call went through. Not waiting to say hello, Brandon hurriedly got to the point.

"Is Frankie there?" he asked anxiously.

"This is Frankie," the person at the other end replied.

"Frankie, I'm so glad to hear your voice. This is Brandon Saunders. Someone apparently backed into my car. The entire back bumper is crushed and barely hanging by a thread. I need you to send a tow truck tonight to take it to your shop."

"Slow down, Mr. Saunders. It's pretty late, can it wait 'til morning?"

Brandon emphatically replied, "No! I have an early morning meeting, and now I don't have a car. It has to be tonight."

He went on a verbal rampage. "Some people don't deserve a driver's license. I was parked in what I thought was a safe neighborhood, and when I returned, I could not believe my eyes."

Frankie allowed him time to vent. After about five minutes, Frankie had his fill; he had no choice but to interrupt him. "Okay Mr. Saunders, don't worry. Someone will be there to get your car, and we'll bring you a loaner," he said.

"Thank you, Frankie. I knew I could depend on you," he replied. "Have them call upstairs when they get here, and I'll be right down with the keys. Right now, I need a stiff drink."

Frankie sighed and said to himself, "If all my customers were like Mr. Saunders, I'd have to see a shrink at least weekly. It's a good thing he pays so well, or I'd drop him like a hot potato."

• • •

The following day, Brandon was in his office by seven o'clock.

Laura was surprised when she arrived at 9:00 and saw him deeply immersed in work.

"Mr. Saunders, did you sleep here last night?" she asked.

He looked up and smiled sweetly. "No, but I had some work I simply couldn't allow another day to pass without completing it. Dr. Sam would have my head."

He clicked off the computer, stood up, and shrugged into his jacket.

"I'm finished here for now. I think I'll go see what's going on out there," he said.

Leaving his office, he wondered if they had found the body of his blackmailer or if by some miracle he had survived. His first stop was the emergency room. It was hectic as usual. Doctors and nurses were running around from one curtained cubicle to another. Multiple cups of coffee, tea, and water were littered on the desk next to vials of blood and urine specimens. Paper charts sprinkled with blood were stacked one on top of the other, not to mention the array of telephones scattered about on every single desk. The phones rang non-stop as stretchers zigzagged down unending corridors, and staff scurried back and forth like worker bees.

"I wonder what Natalie would say if she could see what I'm seeing. I'm really surprised that there are not more infected employees. I have to remember to have a word with her," Brandon said to himself.

The nursing supervisor finally spotted him and came over. "Hi, Mr. Saunders. How can I help you today?" she asked.

"I was just looking around, making sure everything is okay. Now that JCAHO's over, there's a tendency to goof off."

Feigning hurt, she replied, "Mr. Saunders, I'm deeply offended. If there's one place in this hospital where staff doesn't goof off, it's the ER. Just last night they had a multiple gunshot wound brought in that they spent hours trying to revive."

"Really?" replied Brandon. "Were they able to save him?"

"Unfortunately they couldn't, but I know they worked on him for hours."

"I'm sorry to hear. Was this a male or female?"

"Male."

"How old was this person?" Brandon asked.

Looking him up and down, the Supervisor replied, "About your age or a bit older. He looked as if he had a very hard life."

Brandon sighed, "Oh well, another statistic. I hope they find his killer."

With hands in his pockets, he walked away, already wondering how long before his Benz would be ready.

Kirsten Madden

Finally Kirsten had caught Mr. Right. It was the talk of the office and soon the talk of the entire medical center. Charlie Rosen, the medical resident from the Pediatric Department, had lost his heart to Kirsten. Kirsten waltzed into the office flashing the bright, shiny two-carat diamond on her ring finger. The entire staff crowded around trying to get a better look.

"Oh, Kirsten, it's beautiful. When did this happen?" Rochelle gasped.

"Last night," giggled Kirsten, her face glowing all over.

"Well, you finally bagged him, didn't you? You said you only wanted a doctor, and you've got him. You knew what you wanted, and you held out. Good for you. So when's the big day?" asked Rochelle, hugging her tightly.

"We plan to wait until we've saved some more money. Then I'm going to have the wedding of my dreams." Kirsten twirled around, joy radiating all over her beautiful face.

Quite understandably, work was placed on hold for the time being as everyone celebrated Kirsten's good news. However, life goes on, and viruses, bacteria, fungi, and their entire ilk lacked the good sense to wait for the completion of Kirsten's engagement celebration. The incessant ringing of the phone brought everyone back to stark reality.

Quiet descended on the room as Claudine picked up. "Infection Control, how can I help?" she asked.

The person at the other end hesitated. "Hi, Claudine. Is Kirsten there?" she asked.

"Yes," she replied, "and who may I ask is calling?"

"This is Carol, head nurse of the ENT operating room. I need to speak to Kirsten, if you don't mind."

Claudine handed the phone to Kirsten.

"Hi, Carol. How can I help?" Kirsten asked.

"This patient just came up to the OR for a naso-cranial procedure, but he has this rash all over his face that looks like chickenpox. I'm really not sure, but could you come and take a look?"

Kirsten sighed. "Okay, I'll be right up."

It took Kirsten almost two hours to return to the office. During that time, her pager had gone off a minimum of five times. She had returned calls to the bacteriology lab about a new resistant organism on one of her units, returned a call to the Dietary Department regarding the absence of a food refrigerator thermometer, plus a request for the possibility of cohorting two patients with the same resistant organism. And she still had a few more calls to return.

By the time she changed into OR scrubs and started investigating the possible chickenpox exposure, the toll had begun to take its place on her body, and the day was still young.

Returning to the office, she flopped heavily into her desk chair.

"This is some way to remember the day I got engaged," she sighed.

Candace could not help but smile. "Poor, Kirsten. So do you or don't you have an exposure?"

"Yes, I do," moaned Kirsten. "Sadly he was in the holding area along with six other patients, so everyone in that area has been exposed."

"Where is the patient now?" asked Rochelle.

"His surgery was cancelled, and I managed to find the last single room. I placed him on airborne and contact precautions."

As Kirsten talked, she logged on to the computer to obtain the operating room schedule for the day. She was able to download the list of all patients scheduled for surgery between eight and ten o'clock that day. Comparing it with the list she had received from Carol, she was able to begin a search of the exposed patients to determine if any of them had a history of childhood chickenpox or if they had contracted it as adults.

"I hate chickenpox exposures," she said as she continued her search.

What made it difficult to keep track of chickenpox exposures was based on the stage of the rash. It takes between ten and twenty-one days after contact with an infected person for someone to develop chickenpox or varicella, but the average is usually fourteen to sixteen days. This was known as the incubation period.

"Oh, Mr. Ruiz, you have certainly made my day. Why did you choose today of all days to have your surgery and expose these other patients?" Kirsten sighed as she initiated an infection worksheet.

"Not only are your rashes filled with fluid and you're at the most infectious stage, but you have exposed a very immuno-suppressed patient. A patient who's HIV positive, no less," she continued.

"I know it's not your fault," Kirsten continued, "but with the amount of work involved, I just feel that I need to let off some steam. And what better way than to blame someone? Unfortunately it has to be you." She smiled to herself as Candace turned and gave her a questioning look.

Kirsten returned the look. "I'm not crazy, Candace, but you know what I mean. I guess I have to be thankful for small mercies though. Luckily he was admitted two days prior to his surgery, which meant that his initial exposure to chicken pox did not occur here, but in the community. Had it occurred here, that would mean a whole other investigation."

Kirsten spent the rest of the day preparing a list of staff both on the unit where the patient was first admitted, as well as those in the OR that had potentially been exposed. She then faxed the list to the OHS, and then slowly dragged herself out of the office and headed home.

Natalie Sinclair

Returning to work felt so strange. It had only been one day, but the news Natalie had received made it seem like a lifetime since she had been away.

She wondered how she should broach the subject of brain surgery to her staff. After her seizure, she had told them in no uncertain terms that discussion of the subject was off limits. She now realized she might have been a bit harsh while keeping her composure, but little did they know she had been scared to death. She was unsure herself of what was happening, and the thought of having something that would render her incapable of functioning independently, was a very hard pill to swallow.

David had prescribed medication for her headache, but it was having very little effect on the pressure building in her head. The feeling of this constrictive band around her head was constantly present and driving her crazy.

Surgery was scheduled for the following Monday, but David had insisted that she stop working immediately. Steve had wholeheartedly agreed with him and had gotten her solemn promise that today would be her last day at work.

As she alighted from the car she focused all her attention on making it to her office without any untoward incident.

It seems like my condition got worse the moment I received the diagnosis, she thought to herself as she entered the office.

I'm glad I'm caught up on all my projects, so handing over to Candace won't be too stressful for her, she thought.

Candace came in shortly after. She was always so dependable.

As she entered the office, Natalie called out to her. "Hi, Candace. I see you're early. As soon as you're settled, I need to speak with you. Please bring a notebook."

Candace relieved herself of her winter garb then entered Natalie's office, wondering what this early morning summons meant.

You can never tell with her these days, thought Candace.

"Take a seat, please," Natalie invited.

She decided to come straight to the point and get it over before the rest of staff arrived. She would have a meeting with them before the day was over.

"Candace, I won't be here for a while, so I need you to take charge of the department in my absence," Natalie started. "What I'm about to tell you I want to be kept in strict confidence. I will meet with the rest of the staff and update them later."

She took a deep breath and continued before Candace had a chance to ask any questions.

"I saw a neurologist recently and had an MRI. It showed a mass in my brain. That's what caused the seizure that I had some time ago. I'll be having surgery early next week, so I'm leaving you in charge. My doctor wants me to stop working immediately, so today will be my last day."

Without realizing she was speaking rapidly, she quickly released her breath and looked Candace in the eyes.

The shock of her words rendered Candace speechless. Candace wanted to say something, but words had deserted her. She felt like freaking out. Her ears must be deceiving her, but she quickly pulled herself together.

Natalie decided to continue before she too began losing it.

"I don't know how long I'll be gone, but I want to be sure that there is a representative from the department at these meetings," Natalie continued. She opened her desk calendar and flipped through, reviewing the meetings that were scheduled.

After making a few attempts to speak, Candace finally found her voice. She cleared her throat, "Natalie, I'm so sorry, I don't know what to say."

Candace stopped speaking as tears threatened to flow down her cheeks.

"Please don't cry Candace," she said, getting up and closing the office door, not wanting the rest of the staff to see her crying. "I'll start crying if you do. I'll be fine."

Candace took a few deep breaths and regained her self-control.

"I've talked to Ms. Carlyle about giving you a raise and a new title. I think it's overdue, and you deserve it. You've really been a great help to me. I don't say it often, but I do appreciate you, and all that you do." Natalie continued smiling.

The news took Candace completely by surprise. "Thank you, Natalie. I don't know what to say," she stammered.

"Okay, let's continue. If you have a problem that you can't handle, discuss it with each other. If you can't reach a resolution, bring it to Dr. Corbin, and always keep Ms. Carlyle updated on any unusual events. Remember, she's the administrator for the department. Please make sure your reports are submitted on time and review your infections with Dr. Corbin before submitting them to the CDC. I know the staff works independently, but sometimes when the cat is away, the mice will play," Natalie continued.

"Don't forget to reinforce with the nursing staff the new policy of screening for community-acquired MRSA. That goes into effect in two weeks. By this time all nursing staff should've received education on the correct method for collecting the specimens. You'll need to do a demonstration and let them do a return demonstration, so you know everyone's doing it correctly and the data won't be skewed."

"You're talking about the nasal smears, right?" Candace asked.

"Yes. On admission all patients will receive a swab from their nostrils using a Q-tip. This will be repeated on discharge. The admission result will indicate if they were admitted from the community with MRSA. On discharge this will be repeated, and the results will determine if they acquired it in the hospital. Don't forget your isolation precautions, and keep your records current and report all results as per policy. Do you have it all written down, or am I going too fast?"

Candace looked up from her notebook, "No I'm fine. I have it all."

"Review this with the rest of the staff, so you're all on the same page. Everyone should be using the same data collecting forms. This will make it easier for Claudine to do the tallying at the end of the month," Natalie continued.

"I have a number of meetings scheduled for today, so I'll be gone most of the day. I'll meet with the staff after lunch. Please let them know to be present here by 1:30."

Natalie closed her calendar indicating an end to the meeting. She pushed her chair back, and prepared for her first meeting of the day. She did not want to be late, so leaving the office a bit earlier than usual was the only way to accomplish this.

By then the rest of staff had arrived and were busy with their morning schedules. As Candace busied herself with her routine, her mind was on anything but the work at hand.

The rest of the day flew by and soon it was time for Natalie's meeting with the staff. As usual they gathered around the small table in the common area, each wondering what was on the agenda.

They did not have long to wait.

"Ladies," Natalie began. "I'm not going to beat about the bush. I'll come straight to the point. Today will my last day here for a while. I will be having brain surgery next Monday."

You could hear a pin drop.

Natalie continued explaining about the results of her MRI and why Dr. Guthrie needed her to stop working immediately.

"Where will you be having the surgery?" asked Kirsten

"At Kendal Medical Center. My husband works there. They have a wonderful, state of the art Neurology Department there," Natalie replied.

They asked other questions, and Natalie did her best to answer without giving away too much. After all, she knew how things tend to get around Justice, as with all other large institutions, and she wanted to maintain some semblance of privacy.

At the end of the meeting, there was not one dry eye around the table. As she looked around the room, her heart skipped a beat as she realized how much she would miss her staff. They had been through so much together, some good times and some bad; but overall, they were not a bad bunch with which to work.

"I'll really miss you guys," Natalie said, trying hard to hold back the tears.

They all gathered around and hugged her goodbye

Natalie Sinclair

Natalie spent most of Sunday morning lazing about the house being waited on by her family. Admission to the hospital was scheduled for late evening and surgery was for early Monday morning.

"This feels so odd," Natalie complained. "I'm not used to being waited on."

Tristan and Nicole had taken off time from their busy lives to be present for their mother's surgery.

"Enjoy it, Mom. Just think of how much you've done for us. We couldn't let you go through this without being here for you," Nicole piped up. "What kind of kids would we be?" She smiled despite the worry in her voice.

"That's certainly not the way you raised us," said Tristan.

Steve sat next to her on the sofa, hands to his cheek, glancing at his watch every few minutes, not joining in the conversation. The only obvious sign of how much he was deeply worried was the way he constantly wiped at his face and bit his lips. He wanted so desperately to appear strong, the one in charge, the leader of the pack, but his heart had started breaking the moment he had heard the diagnosis. He did not want to think about the outcome of the surgery, because if it was what he feared, then he refused to think about a future without Natalie.

The drive up to Kendal was the quietest they had ever taken as a family, each one deep in their own thoughts. They got Natalie settled into her room, then sat and did small talk.

This is so difficult, Steve thought to himself. *We're not a family who does small talk.*

Soon visiting time was over, and it was time to leave.

"I'm staying the night," Steve announced. "You kids can take the car, and we'll go home together tomorrow."

"No, go home. I'll be fine tonight. I'll see you all tomorrow," said Natalie.

"But what if you need something during the night?" Steve asked sounding desperate. "I should've hired a private nurse like I wanted. I never should've let you talk me out of it," he said with regret in his voice.

"You can still hire her. I'll probably need her after I leave the neurosciences critical care unit (NCCU)."

"Okay, I'll feel so much better," Steve replied.

After much discussion, it was decided that they would all return home and return the next day before Natalie went in to surgery. They all kissed her good-bye and headed home, after ensuring that she was comfortably settled.

At nine o'clock the following morning, the gurney arrived to take Natalie to surgery. Steve and the kids had been in her room for the past hour and were ready for the journey.

Steve kissed her cheeks and squeezed her shoulder. "I'll see you soon. You're in good hands. I love you."

"Love you, Mom," said Tristan, squeezing her hands. "We'll be waiting for you."

"See you soon, Mom. I love you," Nicole smiled at her, fighting hard to hold back the tears.

They were allowed to follow the gurney only to the unrestricted outer doors of the operating room. As the door swung close, they watched through the glass as the gurney continued down the corridor, then turned into operating room number seven, then she was no longer visible to them. For a moment, they all huddled together seeking comfort and solace from each other. Seeming to gather strength from their togetherness, they headed to the waiting area to prepare themselves for the long wait.

Natalie Sinclair

David was dressed in his operating scrubs and waiting for Natalie when she entered the room. As was his practice, before starting a procedure on any of his patients, he made sure he talked with them and offered them reassurance. Today was no different. As a matter of fact, it was even more crucial considering this was the wife of a colleague. So as she entered the room, he headed over to the gurney to welcome his patient.

"Hi, Natalie. Did you sleep well?" he asked.

Natalie nodded. "Yes, I did."

He smiled and squeezed her hands. "Okay, don't worry about a thing. You know I'm going to do my best."

"I know," Natalie replied.

"Do you have any questions?"

Natalie shook her head no and tried smiling, but it did not quite reach her eyes.

One by one, members of the team made their way over to the stretcher to reassure Natalie.

Dr. Guthrie was well known for his high success rate in performing complicated brain surgery. However, from what he had seen on the MRI, he was not sure how long this success rate would continue.

The most important function before the start of any surgical procedure is the surgical scrub. The Association for Professionals in Infection Control (APIC) and the Association of periOperative Registered Nurses (AORN) have recommended that each member of the sterile team perform a hand and arm scrub before entering the surgical suite.

The purpose of surgical hand scrub is to thoroughly remove debris and temporary microorganisms from the nails, hands, and forearms. Hand scrub also helps in reducing the number of resident microorganisms living on hand surfaces and inhibits the rapid re-growth of these microorganisms.

The neuroanesthesiologist had already introduced himself to Natalie and explained what he was about to do. While David was in the process of scrubbing and gowning, the neuroanesthesiologist had inserted several intravenous lines using large bore needles and had connected a number of intravenous fluids.

Natalie was well versed in the steps of surgical hand scrub, and so she trusted David to be thorough. There were never any shortcuts when it came to surgical scrubbing, everyone knew that. However, ever the infection control nurse, just a small part of her wished she could observe his scrubbing technique. She knew that the clock in the scrubbing area was working, having taken a quick glance through the glass door when they wheeled her in. So she had no choice now but to trust that David's integrity would allow him to do the right thing. Fighting a surgical site infection was not something about which she even wanted to think. So she quickly dismissed it from her mind and did her best to relax.

• • •

After completing his gloving, David interlaced his fingers making sure that they fitted perfectly against his fingers. As he did, he offered up a silent prayer: *Dear God, this is one of the most difficult procedures I've ever performed. I humbly ask for your guidance during this time. I'm placing this scalpel in your hands, use it as you see fit. Amen.*

Natalie's head had been shaved and scrubbed, and the site for the proposed incision prepped and draped. Each staff wore a surgical mask over the lower portion of their face, covering their mouths and noses in addition to a protective cap covering their hair.

David approached the operating table. He looked first at the anesthesiologist, and then the nurses. They were anxiously waiting by their stainless steel carts stacked with what looked like hundreds of neatly arranged instruments. He finally turned to the circulating staff, who were ready and waiting to move at the first command.

Their faces were hidden under their masks, so he could not easily determine their facial expressions, but he knew them well; he had worked with them many times before. As his eyes roamed from face to face, he knew they cared deeply for each and every patient that entered these operating rooms.

He would only tolerate the best, and only those who cared.

He also knew they were aware that this was one of their biggest and most difficult challenges. In the end, they would be besieged with tired feet, aching necks and backs because of the long hours of standing, but they would never voice a word of complaint.

David brought his attention back to the anesthesiologist.

"Are we ready?" David asked.

The anesthesiologist nodded yes, and David took his seat on a stool to the right of Natalie's head.

The clock on the wall pointed to ten o'clock. The radio on the corner shelf softly played Peter White's "Promenade" as David made the first incision into the left parietal lobe of Natalie's skull.

Natalie Sinclair

There are varying types of anesthesia that can be used during the performance of brain surgery. Dr. Guthrie and the neuroanesthesiologist had previously discussed and decided the best type of anesthesia for Natalie's tumor removal. Because her tumor lacked clearly defined borders, the choice was made to have her sedated at the beginning and end of the procedure and awake during the middle. The importance of this method was to remove the tumor and avoid damaging other critical parts of the brain.

Surgery has traditionally remained the first line of therapy for patients with primary brain tumors, even though complete surgical removal of some tumors is sometimes not possible. However, even for tumors that cannot be completely removed, surgery can have a major beneficial effect on patients' symptoms and on the effectiveness of other treatments, such as radiation therapy and chemotherapy.

Treatment of gliomas usually involves a multispecialty team. A neuroon-cologist or a doctor who specializes in brain cancers usually heads the team. Other specialists include neurosurgeons, radiation oncologists, medical oncologists, neuroradiologists, and neuropathologists. This was the very best team David had at his disposal, and together they created the best treatment plan appropriate for Natalie's needs.

With input from Steve and Natalie, they devised the best treatment option available. The choices included surgery, radiation therapy and chemotherapy, and the decision had included all the options. So at last, the day and time of surgery was here.

At the appropriate time, the anesthesiologist administered a mild anesthesia for sedation. He then administered a blocking agent that blocked all sensations to that area of the scalp where the team would be working. As Dr. Guthrie made his incision, the neuroanesthesiologist made sure that Natalie remained calm and completely unaware of any pain or discomfort. He continued monitoring her vital signs, including her heart rate, breathing, and blood pressure.

Using one of the specialized instruments, Dr. Guthrie removed a portion of the skull. With the help of his assistant he then dissected the dura mater, the outermost layer of the brain, to expose the tumor. A small portion of the tumor was then resected. This portion was then examined under a microscope by the neuropathologist, who confirmed the diagnosis within ten minutes. The team had hoped against hope that the results would be good, however, this was not the case.

It was malignant. It was cancer.

Natalie was awakened at this time, and David-and the team then resorted to using computer imaging of the brain. Based on Natalie's responses, they created a map of the functional areas of the brain. David then removed all the visible portions of the tumor while trying to avoid damage to the functional areas of the brain. Intraoperative MRI was then utilized to determine whether any residual tumor was present prior to closing the wound. The skull was then replaced and the scalp stitched shut.

It was now eight hours since surgery had begun, and exhaustion was not just making itself felt, but was very evident on the faces of everyone. As Natalie was transferred to the NCCU, David sent up another silent prayer: *Dear God, I thank you for guiding my hands. I did the best that I could. The rest is up to you. Amen.*

Natalie had made it through this portion of her journey, but there was still a long road yet to be traveled. Radiation therapy might prolong her survival, and—who knows—it might even provide a cure in the long run. But for the present time, God had brought her through, and so the rest would be up to Him.

Brandon Saunders 57

To say that Brandon Saunders was a man without a conscience would be putting it mildly. He had already forgotten the little "incident" of the past day and was back to his normal self, whatever "normal" meant for him. The incident was, however, not forgotten by the authorities.

Bright and early the next morning the police detectives were present in the ER asking questions about the patient admitted with the gunshot wounds. This was not unusual for the staff, considering this was a major trauma center, and accidents of all types were usually brought in at all times throughout the day and night. The police detectives were like old friends, quite friendly with both the nursing staff and the doctors. So when Lead Detective Carl Maloney entered the ER and headed toward the head nurses' office, no one's radar went on the alert. It was just another day in the life of a big city trauma center. No one knew that this visit would prove to be very different, and no one anticipated that this visit would eventually lead to the downfall of one of their own.

As Head Nurse Katrina, affectionately called Kat by her colleagues, emerged from her office, she almost caused an accident; the door almost connected with the detective who was attempting to enter her office.

She quickly apologized.

"Why detective, I'm sorry. I didn't see you there! I could've hit you. What are you doing standing at my door?" Kat asked.

Smiling at Kat, on whom he'd had the biggest crush for the longest time, he replied sweetly, "What am I doing here? I came to see you of course."

Kat blushed, "Really? How can I help you?"

"I wanted to see if you would like to have dinner with me?"

"I told you already, I have a boyfriend."

"I don't see a ring on your finger," Detective Maloney said.

"That's not the point. I'm a one-man woman. Anyway, seriously why are you here?"

Hating to switch the conversation, Detective Maloney reluctantly got to the real reason for his visit. Retrieving his well-worn notebook, he flipped a few pages.

"You had a gunshot wound brought in last night. Can you tell me what time he came in?" Detective Maloney asked.

"Well, as you know, I was not here at that time. However, everything you need should be in the admitting log. Let's check and see," Kat said.

She locked her office door, and they both headed toward the main admitting desk. As they passed by the numerous cubicles, the chaos had not diminished in the least; it had increased if anything. But after spending the last ten years in the department, it had become a part of Kat, so she barely noticed. Reaching the main admitting area, she located the large book buried under a barrage of admitting forms and laboratory requests. She flipped through the dog-eared log book, noting that some pages were torn, while others were splattered with old, dried blood. However, she chose to ignore it, and kept turning until she got to the page she wanted.

"Here we are," she said. "He arrived here at 7:00 p.m. He was faintly responsive when his body was discovered. EMS tried to resuscitate him, but they were unsuccessful. They transported the body here, where he was declared dead by our trauma chief and transported to the morgue."

"Can you tell me the cause of death?" asked Detective Maloney.

"Why don't you speak with our trauma chief? He can give you more details." She beckoned to the doctor standing not far off talking to a resident.

"Dr. Simon, Detective Maloney would like some information regarding the gunshot wound from last night."

In an area as chaotic as the ER, where the turnover was fast and high, sometimes a diagnosis was easier to recall than a patient's name. It was not an intentional act of disrespect, but with the sheer number of activities occurring, this was just a coping skill that had developed over time. Dr. Simon finished his discussion and headed toward them.

"How can I help you, Detective?" he asked.

"I'd like to know the cause of death on your patient Rajah Singh who came in last night."

Dr. Simon checked the computer. "Well according to the ME's report, he died almost instantly from the first gunshot to the chest. Both bullets directly penetrated the heart, one slightly above the other. He didn't stand a chance. He was dead shortly after hitting the ground. It appears the shooter wanted to make double sure that he was dead by putting two additional slugs through his brain. Looks like a very angry shooter to me!" He shook his head.

Detective Maloney raised his head after scribbling hurriedly in his notebook. "Is there anything else I should know?" he asked.

Doctor Simon consulted the computer again. "He was infected with the AIDS virus, but there were very high levels of anti-viral drugs in his system, so he definitely was not going to die anytime soon from AIDS."

The detective closed his notebook. "Thank you very much, Doctor."

He looked around for Kat, and spotting her not far off, he headed toward her.

He gave her his usual charming smile. "My offer for dinner still stands. Whenever you're ready, just give me a call."

Kat returned the smile, but did not respond.

Giving her a knowing wink, he headed toward the exit. The automatic doors swung open, and he was soon lost from view.

Natalie Sinclair 58

Natalie surprised everyone with the rapidity of her progress. After surgery, she began the recovery process in the NCCU. She was awake and stable within an hour, and Steve and the children were allowed in to see her. However, because rest was an important component to her recovery, their visit was limited to only ten minutes. She was awake and smiled as she recognized her family, but it was obvious that she was still weak from the surgery. The family also understood that it would take time for her to return to her usual level of energy.

"Hi, Nat," Steve whispered, kissing her on the cheek. She attempted to speak, but he stopped her.

"Don't talk. We just wanted you to know that we're all here. David said that things went very well."

Tristan and Nicole came in, hugged and kissed her, talked to her for a while, and soon it was time for them to leave until the next visiting time.

The team of doctors and nurses in the NCCU were specially trained in neurology and critical care and provided the highest level of intensive, comprehensive care and constant monitoring around the clock. Within a week she was transferred to one of the many neurosurgery nursing units where she would continue her recovery process.

• • •

Surgery for brain tumors can sometimes cause problems with many aspects of a person's behavior. These can include feelings, thoughts and behaviors. Quite often they may need help during the recovery period with different areas of their recovery. Rehabilitation specialists such as physical therapists, occupational therapists and speech language pathologists may be needed to provide assistance.

Physical therapists assess the patient's ability to walk safely and climb stairs before being released from the hospital. They may also help the patient improve strength and balance.

Occupational therapists assess the patient's ability to perform activities of daily living, such as getting dressed, using the toilet, and getting in and out of the shower. They also test the patient's vision and thinking skills to determine whether the patient can return to work, drive a car, or manage other challenging tasks.

If the patient's speech has been affected by the brain tumor, the speech language pathologists will be needed to evaluate problems with speech, language, or thinking. They may also evaluate the patient for disorders or difficulty in eating and swallowing.

Because Natalie's tumor was located on the left side, a minimum amount of disturbance in function was visible on her right side. The main areas of disturbance were located in the areas of vision and motor control. For the first few days, she had some difficulty seeing objects clearly. Grasping objects in her right hand also proved to be a challenge. However, after some intense therapy with both physical and occupational therapists, near to full function was soon regained, and she looked forward to returning home to her family.

As is the policy of all good healthcare facilities, and a requirement of the regulatory bodies, discharge instructions are essential and a part of the total package for all patients. Before being released, the doctors and nurses met with Natalie and her family and went into detailed instructions about home care and what to expect during the healing process. Even though both Steve and Natalie were in the healthcare field, they were not exempt from receiving these instructions. These instructions covered all aspects of her daily activities, including what actions to take in case of an emergency.

Soon the day came for Natalie to go home and despite the old adage that "nurses and doctors make the worse patients," this had not been the case with her. In fact, the entire staff who had participated in her care and recovery was sorry to see her go.

"You've been an excellent patient," said one nurse.

"I wish all our patients were more like you," said another.

"You never used the call bell unless you really needed to," said yet another.

Natalie was so moved by their words, she was finding it difficult to keep from crying. "Thank you all for your wonderful care. You've all been so nice and patient with me. I'm sorry if I tried your patience at times, but I appreciate everything you've done for me. I'll never forget all of you."

"Come back and see us when you're feeling up to it," said the head nurse.

After the hugs and kisses were over, and Steve had settled and buckled her seatbelt, they started home.

Natalie took a deep breath as she looked around at the landscape with tears welling in her eyes. Steve glanced sideways at her.

"Are you okay?" he asked anxiously.

She nodded. "Yes. I was just thinking how close I came to loosing you and the kids. Sometimes we just take so much for granted. This experience is like a second chance for me. From this day forward I promise you, work will take second place to my family. I now realize that not many people get a second chance. I have been granted one, and I will make the most of it the best way I know how."

Her voice choked, as she reached for Steve's hand and squeezed it. They drove on quietly, tears hovering in their eyes. There was no need for words.

Kirsten Madden

Kirsten received a response from OHS the following day. Of the thirteen staff members who had been exposed to the patient with chickenpox, ten showed having immunity either through prior infection or through vaccination. The remaining three showed no history of having immunity to chickenpox. Had they been previously exposed, the immune system would have produced antibodies to the disease. As required by law for each employee, this would have been recorded in their employee health record.

Because of the severity of adult chickenpox exposure, healthcare facilities must ensure that all healthcare workers have evidence of immunity to chickenpox in order to prevent a facility-wide spread of the virus. Not only are employees at risk, but pregnant women and patients with weakened immune systems, especially those with HIV/AIDS, are also at severe risk if they contract the disease.

As she reviewed the results, Kirsten knew she had a few days to play with before these employees had to be furloughed, but full disclosure was the only way to go. She did not want a delay in informing the affected area of the results. They deserved to have the information in hand so that they would have adequate time to make the necessary changes she knew this information would engender.

Based on policy, all employees without documented evidence of immunity or vaccination are potentially infectious from day ten through day twenty-one after exposure. Not all exposures usually result in infection, but this was one infectious disease that did not afford you the luxury of ignorance.

Nursing staff shortage is nothing new to healthcare facilities, and Justice Medical was no different. Kirsten knew she had no choice but to inform Carol that it was imperative that these staff members be furloughed on the tenth day after exposure and remain off duty for twelve days. However, before furlough, they would be administered the chickenpox or varicella vaccine following Department of Health guidelines.

Kirsten headed out to the OR. As she changed into scrubs, she started thinking of how she would broach the subject with the head nurse. Carol could be reasonable when she wanted to be, but Kirsten knew that this was the type of news Carol did not want to hear.

Putting on her diplomatic hat, she approached Carol. She slipped on her best smile, and waved, "Hey, Carol. How's it going?" Getting the informal small talk out of the way was crucial, so Kirsten waded right in.

"Okay," replied Carol. She paused, looking at Kirsten suspiciously.

She had never been very friendly with Kirsten. In Carol's mind she knew Kirsten wanted what was best for both patients and staff, and so did she, but sometimes infection control just seemed so inconvenient.

"After all, who can afford to follow the rules to the letter all the time?" Carol has asked herself more than once.

"I've never seen you here this early. Do you have bad news for me?" Carol asked.

Busted, thought Kirsten, but this was the name of the game. Sometimes the news was not always good, but someone had to deliver it anyway. It all came down to the health and safety of both staff and patients, so being the bad guy once in a while was all par for the course.

"Well," Kirsten replied, "three of your staff have no history of chickenpox, so they need to be furloughed on day ten through day twenty-one."

Kirsten held her breath waiting for the unleashing of the tornado.

She did not have long to wait.

Carol's entire appearance changed before Kirsten's very eyes.

"What? Three nurses for twelve days? You're kidding. Do you know how many cases we have scheduled for those days? What am I supposed to tell the doctors? These cases have been booked for months," she yelled.

"I'm sure they will understand once they hear the problem," Kirsten said.

Carol fumed as she paced, but nothing she did would alter the situation. Kirsten was not budging. This was not something she controlled or could change on a whim. This was the policy, and no one could change it.

Realizing she was outmanned, Carol gave in. "Who am I to fight with Infection Control? We might have to cancel some cases. Are you going to tell the doctors?"

"Don't worry. I'll take care of it," replied Carol.

She exited the OR and sighed, "One battle won, so many more to go."

• • •

The source patient remained isolated on airborne precautions and contact precautions in addition to standard precautions. Adhering to approved policy, he would remain on isolation in a negative pressure room until all his lesions were dry and crusted. During this time, he would not be allowed any visitors who did not have evidence of immunity to chickenpox or cared for by staff having no evidence of immunity.

The physicians for the six patients who were exposed had all been notified. Blood specimens were obtained and all had positive IgG ELISA, indicating the presence of antibodies to chickenpox, either from past disease history or vaccination.

Kirsten breathed a sigh of relief on hearing the news, thankful it would be one less road she would need to travel.

Candace Roberts 60

"I hate going to these meetings," Candace mumbled to herself as she collected documents from Natalie's desk to prepare for her meeting. "I have no idea how to read a blueprint. I'm a nurse for God's sake, not an engineer."

"Candace, are you talking to yourself again?" Rochelle called out, trying her best not to laugh.

"Yes, I am talking to myself, Rochelle. Would you like to go to this construction meeting for me?"

"Me? No thank you. What's this all about anyway?"

"They're renovating the single rooms on ward five to accommodate patients needing airborne isolation."

"Oh, that should be easy," replied Rochelle snidely.

"Easy?" Candace replied heatedly. "If it's so easy, then why don't you go?"

"You're the one Natalie left in charge, Ms. Assistant Director," retorted Rochelle, the envy obvious in her voice.

"Oh, Rochelle, it's just a title. I have no autonomy. I still have my same assignment. I still do the same work as I did before, so please don't go there," returned Candace heatedly.

Realizing she needed to get away before a full-fledged argument erupted, Candace gathered her documents and left the office.

By the time she reached the conference room in the next building, some of her steam had evaporated. She sincerely hoped she'd be able to focus. However, as she entered the conference room she could feel the tightness in her stomach returning. Although she had used her strongest antiperspirant, she could feel herself starting to perspire. All the chairs around the table were occupied, so she headed to the last vacant chair at the back of the room. Several of those present greeted her as she took her seat.

After the attendees introduced themselves, the meeting got underway.

"We're here to discuss the renovation of the negative pressure rooms on ward five. To recap, there are six rooms located at the western end of the unit, and these are to be brought up to code to house active TB patients. As required by the Department of Health, these rooms must have..." Looking around the table, Mr. Carson, the chairperson asked, "Candace, can you please bring us up to speed and explain what the requirements are for these rooms? I know Natalie's out sick."

All heads turned to face Candace.

Candace was in her element. This was her platform, and she had every intention of making herself heard. All signs of nervousness disappeared as she launched into her favorite subject.

She started out bold. Her voice was well modulated, no tremors in her voice, she radiated confidence.

"All those who thought I didn't deserve that promotion, here's my chance to prove you wrong," she said to herself as she got to her feet.

"Okay. As Mr. Carson stated, these rooms will be converted into *negative pressure* rooms. This is an isolation technique used to prevent cross-contamination from one room to another. Negative pressure rooms require a ventilation system that removes contaminated air from a room. This system allows air to flow into the isolation room but not escape from the room. This technique is required for isolation of patients with contagious diseases that are transmitted by airborne route such as tuberculosis, chickenpox, or measles.

"There should be a minimum of twelve air changes per hour, and the doors should be self-closing. The isolation rooms should be at least twenty-five feet from other ventilation intakes or occupied areas, and the bathroom should also be at negative pressure with respect to the isolation room. The system must have removable HEPA-filters and a schedule for changing these filters."

A hand went up from the audience. Candace acknowledged.

"Who would be responsible for changing these filters, Candace?"

"This is usually the responsibility of the Engineering Department," replied Candace, turning to face Mr. Carson. Heads nodded as she returned to her presentation.

"There should be a half-inch gap under the door to allow for intake of clean air, and except for this gap, the room should be as airtight as possible. Leakage from any unsealed sources or spaces within the room can compromise or eliminate room negative pressure.

"In addition, there must be an ante-room which should be under positive pressure with respect to the inner room where the patient will be housed."

As Candace paused for breath to gather momentum, Mr. Carson held up his hand.

"Candace, is there a lot more to be covered?" he drawled.

Knowing she had the other attendees eating out of the palm of her hands, she smiled and replied. "Not much more, but this part is very important."

"Okay, go ahead," Mr. Carson said resignedly.

Picking up where she left off, Candace continued, "The room must have multiple outlets for oxygen, a mechanical ventilator, and last but not least, a hand washing sink in the ante-room.

"It must have an alarm system that will sound if the room pressure falls below the desired reference pressure range, and of course, there must be an audible alarm to alert nursing staff when this happens. And last but by no means least, a log must be maintained by both nursing and engineering departments for daily recording of the pressure readings."

Candace knew she had done an excellent job, but she kept her joy hidden.

"Thank you, Candace," replied Mr. Carson.

Looking at his watch, he sighed. "It seems we're almost out of time. Are there any questions regarding what Candace just said?"

"Yes, I have just one," asked an attendee. "What happens if and when this alarm sounds?"

Before resuming her seat, Candace replied, "Nursing will inform the engineering department that this is occurring, and a qualified person should be sent to do an inspection. The longer they take to respond, the greater the chance of an exposure to others."

"That was so very thorough. Thank you, Candace," responded another attendee.

"That's true," mumbled Mr. Carson. "Okay, meeting adjourned. We'll call another meeting as things continue to progress."

As chairs scraped on the hardwood floor and papers rustled in preparation to exit the room, Candace quietly slipped out. As she made her way down the corridor, she couldn't help but give a vigorous fist pump, as she realized that she had just given a stellar performance and all her previous anxieties had been totally unnecessary.

Detective Maloney

61

As Detective Maloney headed out the door, he was just in time to see one of the detectives from his team headed toward the office of the hospital administrator.

"Hold up, Griffin," he called out. "Where are you heading?"

"Boss, I just got a tip about a car that was seen speeding away from the site near the shooting. It was described as a black Benz with New York plates. The eyewitness said that it backed into a white car that was parked directly behind it. I'm also told that one of the administrators…" he paused and consulted his notes, "a Mr. Saunders owns a black Benz."

"I'll come with you," replied detective Maloney.

Getting to Brandon's office, which was located in another building at the end of the campus, took some time, but it was eventually located and they headed upstairs to locate him.

In response to their knock, the office door was opened by Brandon's secretary. From just one look, Laura quickly determined they were from law enforcement.

"Good morning, gentlemen. How can I help you today?" Laura asked.

"I'm Detective Maloney, and this is Detective Griffin," he said motioning to his partner. "Is Mr. Saunders in?"

"Yes he is. I'm his secretary. May I ask what this is about?"

"Does Mr. Saunders own a black Mercedes Benz?"

"I believe he does. Is something wrong officers? Maybe I can help?" she replied hesitantly.

"We would rather speak directly with Mr. Saunders if you don't mind," replied Detective Maloney.

Reluctantly Laura turned and headed for Brandon's office. The door to his office was slightly ajar, so Laura knocked and poked her head in.

"Mr. Saunders, there are two detectives here to see you. They won't tell me what they want. They want to speak with you."

Brandon's heart skipped a beat. He looked up from the document he was reading and smiled. "Show them right in, Laura. Don't keep the officers waiting."

As the detectives entered his office, Brandon could feel the butterflies in his stomach working overtime, but he tamped them down.

Never let them see you sweat, one of his favorite mottos, came to mind.

"Gentlemen, please have a seat. How can I help you today?" he asked.

"Do you own a black Mercedes Benz, Mr. Saunders?"

"Yes, I do. As a matter of fact, someone damaged my bumper last night. It's presently in the garage being repaired."

"Where were you parked when it got damaged?" asked Detective Griffin.

"At Maroni's restaurant, just across the street," replied Brandon.

"What time was this?"

Brandon tried to look thoughtful, "Around five—six o'clock."

"Is this some place where you normally hang out?" asked Detective Maloney.

Brandon looked at him askance, gave a smirk, and replied, "Well, I don't exactly 'hang out,' Detective, but I occasionally go there after a stressful work day. However, I hear that a lot of employees from Justice go there after work."

"So did you drive your Benz in to work today?" asked Detective Griffin.

"No, I didn't. I hate driving it when it's not in pristine condition. You know how it is, Detective. You are what you drive. It's in the garage as we speak."

Brandon laughed heartily at his own joke, hoping they would also see the humor.

"So what's the name of the garage where your car is being repaired?" Detective Griffin continued.

"It's called 'The Third Garage.' It's located on Third and Forty-Second Streets. You can't miss it."

Detective Griffin wrote the name down and the questioning continued. After several more questions that were not yielding the answers they wanted, the detectives decided to take a different approach. They had practiced a million times before, so when they gave each other the signal, it was go time.

Detective Maloney started the game.

"So Mr. Saunders, what's the name of the person you were meeting with at Maroni's?" he asked conspiratorially.

Brandon gave a start. "Who said I was meeting with someone?" He could barely keep his voice steady.

"Why are you asking him that? He never said he met with anyone," Detective Griffin piped up, looking with feigned disgust at his partner.

"Maybe, just maybe, he ran into an old friend," replied Detective Maloney. "And maybe they had an argument, and maybe it just escalated...got out of hand. I'm just saying."

Detective Maloney started slowly pacing around the room, a definite change in his demeanor. Suddenly he whirled on Brandon.

"Who was the friend you met with, Mr. Saunders, and what was the argument about?" he yelled.

Brandon almost jumped out of his skin.

"I didn't mean to kill him," he blubbered, falling to his knees. "It was an accident. He wanted to take away everything I have worked so hard for."

"An accident?" yelled Detective Maloney. "You shot him four times! This was premeditated!"

By now Detective Griffin had produced his handcuffs and was about to apply them to Brandon's wrist, but Brandon had no intention of making it easy for him. Summoning all his strength, he leaped across his desk, and reached into his desk drawer. He came up with a .45 and pointed at the detectives.

By now Laura was drawn to the commotion, and approaching the office door, she was just in time to see Brandon raise the gun. In a voice she scarcely recognized as Brandon's, she heard, "Detectives, I'm sorry to disappoint you, but I can't allow you to take me out of here alive. I am Brandon Saunders, and you have no idea what I've been through to get this far. How would you like it if someone tried to take away everything you've labored for all your life?"

By this time his eyes were wild and feral as he looked from one detective to the other. He was barely recognizable as the dapper hospital administrator with the penchant for beautiful women. Even his well-coiffed hair had become disheveled.

Laura's breath hitched in her throat as she ran back to her office and quickly dialed Dr. Sam's office.

The phone was picked up on the second ring. Quickly Laura explained the situation, and Dr. Sam came on the line.

"Laura, stay calm. I'll be right there. I'm bringing hospital security." Before Laura had time to reply he had hung up.

By this time the noise in Brandon's office had escalated, as the detectives tried to talk him out of doing the obvious. Laura ran back to see what was happening. Suddenly it all became very calm. Brandon was standing in a corner with the gun pointed at his head. He was so calm, it was eerie. Laura knew him well, and she did not like what she was seeing.

As she entered the room, their eyes connected. They seemed to say, "I'm sorry Laura, but I need to do this. I wasn't made for prison. I would never survive."

Their eyes lingered for what seemed an eternity, and then everything seemed to be moving in slow motion as the blast from the gun echoed through the room.

The office door burst open and a group, headed by Dr. Sam, entered. Slowly Brandon's body slid to the floor.

"You're too late," sobbed Laura. "You're too late."

Natalie Sinclair

Time flew by on wings, and Natalie had been busy with her physiotherapy and occupational therapy sessions. The sessions had gone extremely well and she had responded quicker than expected. It was now three months since she had had brain surgery and she was getting extremely antsy to return to work. She had not made her wishes known, but Steve had watched her daily and knew her well enough to know what she was thinking. However, he told himself that he would not broach the subject, but would patiently wait until she was ready to discuss it.

Arriving at work the following day, he went in search of David. He did not feel like small talk, so he came straight to the point.

"David, I think Natalie wants to return to work."

David looked him in the eyes and smiled.

"Well good morning to you too Steve." Steve did not return his smile, and David knew him well enough to know when he was worried, so he quickly put on his professional face.

"Well I saw her last week for her checkup, she never mentioned that," David replied. "Has she said as much to you, or are you assuming this is what she wants?"

"No, but I know my wife. She won't mention it, but I can feel it. What's your opinion? Is she ready?"

David took a deep breath. "She has come a long way, much better and much faster than I anticipated, but she's still not out of the woods." He was in deep thought for a while.

Suddenly he responded, "I tell you what, at her next appointment, which is next Monday, we'll discuss the subject. If she is determined, and depending on my findings, I have no objections with her returning to work on a part-time basis. How do you feel about that?"

Steve smiled. "Sounds like music to my ears."

They shook hands and parted, Steve's heart feeling much lighter than when he had first entered.

Natalie Sinclair

Monday was here before she knew it, and Natalie had received the green light from David to return to work. She was on cloud nine after receiving the good news. Not wanting to break her high spirits, Steve allowed her to drive home from the appointment. After driving a short distance on the usual route, Natalie decided to take a different way home.

"Where are we going?" asked Steve suddenly feeling nervous.

"Well, I'm in such a good mood, I feel like going shopping. Now that I'm going back to work, I'd like to look better than when I left," she said with a smile.

"Okay, if it makes you happy," replied Steve.

The week seemed to fly by on wings. Natalie had been in touch with Ms. Carlyle, the department head, and all the required documents had been submitted to human resources. She had been seen and granted medical clearance by OHS to return to work and she had taken care of all the other things that were required.

Soon Monday morning finally arrived. Natalie felt a fleeting sense of anxiety, but this was only temporary. Even though she was reluctant to admit it to herself, she had missed her staff. She hoped they had missed her too.

That feeling of exhilaration soon overcame her as she got behind the wheel of her car and headed down the highway. The angels must have been smiling down on her as she made the easy trek into work. She thought she would be the first to arrive as usual, but that was not about to happen today.

As she headed down the long, dark, dingy corridor she realized that nothing had changed. She knew the staff was expecting her, but beyond that, she would just take it one step at a time. After all, she was only back working on a part time basis for now, so she planned to limit any major involvement and allow Candace to continue in her role as the one in charge. As she approached the door to the office, she noticed the light was on.

"I guess they forgot to turn the lights off when they left on Friday," she said to herself as she slowly inserted the key into the lock. It was so quiet and lifeless. "I almost forgot this feeling. I can't say I missed this part."

"Surprise!"

Natalie almost fainted as people started streaming from the offices and the small kitchen into the main room with open arms, reaching out to hug her. Wasting no time, Candace led her by the hand into the nearby conference room. As she entered, another huge cheer erupted from those anxiously awaiting her return.

The conference room was decorated with colorful banners, streamers, and balloons, all welcoming her back. There were large tables overflowing with all kinds of breakfast foods. Every department was represented, and the sound of celebration was audible all around:

"Welcome back, Natalie. Glad to have you back."

"We missed you. It's so good to see you."

"You were really missed."

Natalie was speechless, but she managed to hide the tears well. Her smile said it all.

She was back where she belonged.

Glossary

Infection Control is the discipline concerned with preventing nosocomial or healthcare-associated infections. It refers to policies and procedures used to minimize the risk of spreading infections, especially in acute care hospitals, long-term care facilities, Outpatient Clinics, and animal health care facilities.

The goals of infection control programs are many. However, they all strive toward obtaining the same positive outcomes.

The major goals include:

1. Protecting the patient.
2. Protecting the health care workers, visitors, and all others in the environment.
3. Defining precautions that can prevent exposure to potentially infectious agents, and restricting the exposure of health care workers to infectious agents.
4. Immunizing against preventable diseases.

An Infection Control Manager or Director is a specially trained professional, oftentimes a nurse, who oversees infection control programs.

An Infection Control Nurse (ICN) or Infection Control Practitioner (ICP) is a registered nurse assigned responsibility for surveillance and infection prevention, education, and control activities.

Some of the commonly recommended precautions to prevent and control the spread of infections include (but are not limited to):

1. Frequent hand washing or use of hand hygiene gels or foams
2. Use of antibiotics only as directed by a physician.
3. Appropriate use of personal protective equipment (PPE) by healthcare workers.
4. Appropriate isolation of potentially infectious patients.
5. Appropriate disposal of infected or potentially infectious materials.

All guidelines and recommendations for the control of infection in healthcare settings were provided by the Centers for Disease Control and Prevention (CDC) and the Healthcare Infection Control Practices Advisory Committee (HICPAC).

Key Places

CDC
The Centers for Disease Control and Prevention (CDC) is the US agency charged with tracking and investigating public health trends. The stated mission of the CDC is: "To promote health and quality of life by preventing and controlling disease, injury, and disability." The CDC is a part of the U.S. Public Health Services (PHS) under the Department of Health and Human Services (HHS).
www.cdc.gov

HICPAC
Healthcare Infection Control Practices Advisory Committee (HICPAC) is a federal advisory committee made up of fourteen external infection control experts who provide advice and guidance to the Centers for Disease Control and Prevention (CDC) and the secretary of the Department of Health and Human Services (HHS) regarding the practice of health care infection control, strategies for surveillance and prevention, and control of health care associated infections in United States health care facilities. One of the primary functions of the committee is to issue recommendations for preventing and controlling health care associated infections in the form of guidelines, resolutions, and informal communications.
www.cdc.gov/hicpac/

JCAHO
The Joint Commission on Accreditation of Healthcare Organizations is a private, not for profit organization established in 1951 to evaluate health care organizations that voluntarily seek accreditation. The Joint Commission evaluates and accredits more than 16,000 health care organizations in the United States, including 4,400 hospitals, more than 3,900 home care entities, and over 7,000

other health care organizations that provide behavioral health care, laboratory, ambulatory care, and long term care services. The Joint Commission also evaluates and accredits health plans and health care networks. It is governed by representatives from the American College of Physicians, the American College of Surgeons, the American Dental Association, the American Hospital Association, the American Medical Association, an at-large nursing representative, six public members, and the Joint Commission President. www.jcaho.org

OSHA

Occupational Safety and Health Administration (OSHA) is a federal organization (part of the Department of Labor) that ensures safe and healthy working conditions for Americans by enforcing standards and providing workplace safety training.

Created in response to the Occupational Safety and Health Act of 1970, OSHA's main goal is to protect the rights and safety of workers by preventing workplace injuries and deaths and holding employers accountable for safe workplaces. OSHA provides workers and employers with information about hazardous working conditions and they offer free assessment for workplace dangers.

There is a strict set of federal safety standards to which all businesses must adhere. These regulations cover things like disposal of hazardous materials, required personal safety equipment such as safety goggles, permitted noise levels and fall protection. OSHA inspects workplaces to ensure they're following all regulations to reduce chances of accident or injury.www.osha.gov

For a complete list of Infection Control Guidelines and Recommendations, please refer to the websites of the aforementioned organizations.